THE FINAL STROLL ON PERSEUS'S ARM

PERSEUS GATE: ORION SPACE – BOOK 6

BY M. D. COOPER

SPECIAL THANKS

Just in Time (JIT) & Beta Reads

Manie Kilian
David Wilson
Marti Panikkar
Scott Reid
Lisa Richman
Jim Dean
Belxjander Serechai
Timothy Van Oosterwyk Bruyn

Cover Art by Andrew Dobell
Editing by Tee Ayer

Edition 1.02

TABLE OF CONTENTS

FOREWORD

Back in March of 2017, I thought I was getting close to completing New Canaan and came to a startling realization: I had another book's worth of novel to write before the story was done.

However, that was going to be problematic as the pre-order was slated to be delivered on April 1, and Amazon is not forgiving of missed pre-order dates.

What's more, New Canaan was already (and still is, to this date) the longest book I'd ever written. There was no way I could add in the additional content and get the book edited and proofed in time.

I decided to take a part of the book out and separate it into the story you now know as Perseus Gate: Orion Space.

Something I considered doing was to write what is The Gate at the Grey Wolf Star story, and then this final episode (The Final Stroll on Perseus's Arm), combine them into one, and then produce it as a standalone novel.

But I'd also been thinking of something else. Some of my favorite TV shows over the years have been ones that had a core cast of characters that got to go on a new adventure every episode.

Shows like the original Star Trek, Dr. Who, and Stargate SG1 are examples of shows that captured this format very well. I wanted to tell stories like that, showing a more up-close view of the wild and varied places humans live in the far future, as well as reveal more about the crew of *Sabrina* than I would get to in a single novel.

And so I set out on this great adventure to tell you the story of *Sabrina*'s journey through Orion Space back to New Canaan. I had no idea how much I'd enjoy telling these stories; I know from the feedback I've received, that some of you consider the Perseus Gate stories (though they are shorter reads) to be some of your favorite Aeon 14 tales.

But now we're coming to the end of Season 1, which I've taken to calling the 'Orion Space' season, and that means the final story before *Sabrina* arrives at New Canaan.

If you've read the book, New Canaan, you'll recall that *Sabrina* appeared at the very end of the story, jumping into the New Canaan System right after Tanis stormed the bridge of the *Galadrial*, the Transcend President's flagship.

Many of you (with self-control that I find to be very impressive) have held off reading Orion Rising because you don't want to be spoiled (as I warned that book does). When you've read this story, you'll be able to sally forth and tackle Orion Rising, and move on through the series.

For those of you who have read Orion Rising, this tale will contain some things you already know, but I suspect it will give you renewed hope for the future.

Finally, once you've read this story *and* Orion Rising, you'll be able to dive into the next Perseus Gate series, entitled: Perseus Gate: Inner Stars. The first book of which will be A Meeting of Minds and Bodies, coming in February 2018.

With that aside, let's dive in and read about the crew's final stroll on Perseus's arm....

M. D. Cooper
Danvers, 2017

PREVIOUSLY IN ORION SPACE...

It has been nine years since Jessica flew *Sabrina* through the jump gate at the Grey Wolf Star, sending the ship and crew across known space, and into the Perseus Arm of the galaxy.

Once there, the crew found themselves at the edge of the Orion Freedom Alliance. Indeed, they found themselves at the edge of settled space itself.

Much of what the crew went through in the Perseus Arm was the result of Jessica's run-in with a diminutive debutante named Phoebe on Hermes Station in the Naga System.

It was there that Jessica became Retyna Girl and gained her photoluminescent skin, where the crew learned of RHY Dynamics' bioweapon, and where they subsequently destroyed the planet Marsalla.

Those events set in motion a chain reaction, with Mandy and Jenn learning of *Sabrina*'s advanced shielding, their telling Derrick of the ship's tech, and the subsequent abduction of Jessica and Cheeky.

That brought them to Serenity, and from there to Star City.

At Star City, Jessica, Iris, and Trevor created sixteen AI children who they have left in charge of the massive dyson sphere. Jessica still has every intention of returning some day, but for now she knows they must return Finaeus to New Canaan.

From Star City, the crew took *Sabrina* through the path in the clouds, an FTL corridor through the Stillwater Nebula that shaved over a year off their journey back to New Canaan.

There they encountered the Perry Strait and liberated a people from oppression before continuing on their way.

Once past the Stillwater Nebula, the crew began to make good time through the stars, continuing to pose as a starfreighter establishing new trade routes.

Over the ensuing eight years, they worked their way into the gap between the Perseus and Orion arms of the galaxy, and are now in a region of space that is only a few hundred light years from the unsettled spaces between the Orion Freedom Alliance and the Inner Stars.

The crew refers to this region of space as the 'retro-zone' where advanced technology is sequestered, and care is taken not to alert the Inner Stars civilizations to the presence of settled space this far from Sol.

Sabrina's route has brought them to a system named Sullus where they have a delivery to make on a planet named Ferra. The crew lands *Sabrina* on the world's surface, where they decide to enjoy a much-needed vacation while waiting for their next shipment to be readied....

PLANETSIDE

STELLAR DATE: 03.10.8948 (Adjusted Years)
LOCATION: Outskirts of Parda City, Ferra, Sullus System
REGION: Midway Cluster, Orion Freedom Alliance Space

Eight years after passing through the Stillwater Nebula…

Nance collected the table's drinks from the bar and carried them back to where Cargo and Trevor sat.

She placed the beverages before the men, rattling off the names as each glass settled before its owner. "Whiskey on the rocks for you, Cargo. Bourbon for you, Trevor. And a delicious chocolate martini for me."

"You always take the risks," Trevor said as Nance sat.

"What do you mean?" Nance asked as she lifted her martini.

"The drinks. You always go for something that could end badly."

Cargo nodded. "He's right. Martinis are a risk. There's too much stuff in them. Half these systems can't tell a watermelon from a cumquat. You sure you know what they're putting in your drink?"

"I'm not sure *I* even know what a cumquat is," Nance replied. "But seriously, it's a chocolate liquor, a few types of cream, and vodka."

"I see two problems with that," Cargo said to Trevor. "You?"

"Three."

Nance gave a soft laugh and shook her head at the two men.

Though she was one of the three women aboard *Sabrina*, she usually preferred to hang out with the guys. It wasn't that Nance had anything against Jessica and Cheeky. They were two of her best friends; they just didn't share many interests.

For starters, both of them *loved* fashion—which she could appreciate—but Nance only needed so many outfits. She was certain Jessica and Cheeky—given enough time—could purchase enough clothing that the mass would eventually slow the local expansion of the universe.

At least Cheeky was a moderately stabilizing influence. Left to her own devices, Jessica would return with bags of clothing—purple more often than not—and guns. Jessica *loved* to buy a new gun. Over the years of their journey through the Perseus Arm, Jessica had bought a weapon on nearly every stop.

She claimed it was for research, but no one believed her.

Cheeky had gained a more nuanced appreciation for weaponry, but she tended toward small, but deadly options. A necessity with the outfits she wore.

Given the choice of going on a shopping spree with the two of them—talking guns and how they went with a particular jacket—scouring the markets with Misha and Finaeus, or having a couple of drinks at a local watering hole, Nance would pick drinks with the guys every time.

Trevor and Cargo were arguing as to whether or not the disparate creams could be counted as separate risks in her drink. Cargo said 'No', but Trevor was aiming for 'Yes'.

"What if the cows have the wrong number of nipples here on Ferra?" Trevor asked. "We saw that back…shit, I forget where, but I know we saw weird double-uddered cows somewhere. Milk there tasted way off."

"OK, OK." Cargo raised his hands in defeat. "I'll grant you that cows are suspect. It could be four issues."

"You guys set then?" Nance asked. "Lay 'em on me."

"OK, cows first," Trevor said. "Number of nipples notwithstanding, they eat different stuff everywhere. Makes any cream product a risk. You've got weird creamy liqueur stuff, *and* straight up cream in your drink. Double risk for nasty tastin's there."

"Go on," Nance said with a smile as she held her drink and breathed in its vodka-laced chocolate aroma.

"The chocolate is your next issue," Cargo said. "Where do they grow it? How do they process the beans? What additives are in it? Who knows? It's a crapshoot. We've been to a lot of places where the chocolate tasted like ass."

"Well, I don't know about ass," Trevor countered.

"Really?" Cargo pressed. "You remember Nippawan Station? Ass, Trevor, the chocolate there tasted like ass."

"Huh, yeah, you're right," Trevor said as he nodded thoughtfully. "I do recall that now. OK, ass chocolate is a double risk."

"Lastly, we've got the vodka itself," Cargo said, spreading his hands wide. "We all know that vodka is made from potatoes. But not just any potato. It has to be the right type in the right soil, and that's just the beginning."

Nance's eyes darted from Cargo to Trevor, a smile on her lips. "So, let me get this straight. Cream is a double risk because of grass varieties and cows with too many nipples." The men were nodding at this point. "Chocolate is another double risk because it can taste bad, *and* it can also taste like ass—based on one station."

"It *really* tasted like ass," Cargo said. "Seems prudent to double-risk that one."

"OK, I'll buy that," Nance agreed. "Not into ass taste at all here. Lastly we're looking at the risk of an incorrect source plant for vodka, and/or wrong type of potato. Was that a double or single risk? I didn't follow that part."

Trevor nodded resolutely. "I say double. They could be making it from something stupid like watermelon, or they could also just generally screw it up."

A candy cane had accompanied her drink, and Nance swirled the sweet stick in the creamy liquid.

"The candy cane a risk?"

Cargo and Trevor looked at each other and shrugged.

"Naaaah," Trevor said with a grin. "We'll give you a bye on the candy cane.

"Six-X threat," Nance mused. "All in this little drink."

"Remember," Cargo said with a grin. "Cow nipples and ass tasting chocolate."

Nance took another deep breath. "Pretty sure that we're safe from ass taste here, boys."

She gave them both a long look, drew in a deep breath, pretended to reconsider the drink, and then downed it in two seconds flat.

"Hoooooo!" Trevor shouted while Cargo banged a fist on the table.

"Look at you!" Cargo high-fived Nance. "Dirt-side, wearing fabric clothing that *anything* could crawl through, drinking at a dive bar, and taking on a six-x threat! Who are you, and what have you done with Nance?"

She gave a warm smile, knowing he meant nothing by it, but not so sure if his statement was that far off.

The advanced nanotech helping her ensure her body was clean and well managed—the only thing keeping her extreme germaphobia at bay, and giving her the confidence to drink a martini in a bar with all those risks attached—had come with a price.

A thing that lived inside her somewhere.

Over the years she'd taken to calling it the 'remnant'. That's what it seemed like to her. A remnant of the thing she had met on Ikoden station. Like a sliver or a shard left inside her mind.

It had been dormant for years, but every now and then, she felt a stirring from it.

Like she felt this very day.

Nance had a feeling the remnant wanted something. She wasn't certain what, but knew the thing would make its desires known at the least opportune time.

"I tell yah," Cargo said as he leaned back in his chair and folded his hands behind his head. "This is the life.

Plying the black, trading in whatever comes our way, and having time for some relaxation with friends."

"Despite where we are?" Trevor asked.

Cargo shrugged. "Doesn't matter where we are. So long as there's a black sky to fly *Sabrina* in."

Nance laughed softly. "Look at you, waxing poetic. Don't you ever want to settle down?"

"Someday." Cargo nodded slowly and took a sip of his drink. "I'd like to raise animals planetside. Horses, maybe."

"That's a far cry from the current day job," Trever observed.

"Yeah, but that's the point. If I change up, I want to really change it up."

"Starships to horseshit, that's a change alright," Nance said as she raised her empty glass. "To Cargo shoveling manure in his dotage."

The men laughed and met her toast and took a drink, each with a thousand-meter stare as they thought about what they'd do when this journey was finally over.

* * * * *

Jessica snorted a laugh. "Cheeks, you look ridiculous in that hat. Who would have thought a cow-town like this would have such weird stuff?"

Cheeky stood, hands on hips, and cocked her head to the side, a wide grin on her face. "I think it's awesome! It's like my head's just a big bubble!"

She was right, the hat was essentially a big pink bubble that came down past the wearer's nose. When

Cheeky had pulled it over her head, the thing had drawn her hair out two holes giving her bubble-head a pair of pig-tails.

"Does it have cameras, or are you using probes to see?"

"Kickin' it old-school, Jess. This thing has little screens in front of my eyes. Not sure where the cameras are, a bit higher than my eyes, I think."

<It's really low res,> Piya complained. *<You're going to give me a headache looking at that.>*

"So don't look." Cheeky grinned—which looked strange since her mouth was all Jessica could see.

"So are you gonna buy it or what?" Jessica asked.

"Think Cargo would have a conniption if I tried to fly the ship wearing it?" Cheeky asked, bobbing her head side to side.

Jessica sighed and shook her head. "I doubt he'd even let you on the bridge with that thing on. Take it off so that we can go somewhere else."

Cheeky pulled the hat off and set it back on the shelf. "Jess, you ruin all my fun. You just want to get back in the sunlight so you can bask in it like the weirdo you are."

Jessica would have taken umbrage with Cheeky's statement, except it was true, she *was* really eager to get out into the sunlight.

The Sullus System's star was a delicious G-spectrum orb. The planet's atmosphere was thick enough to filter out the harmful bands and give her the EM spectrum she craved.

Cheeky, on the other hand, claimed the light was going crack her precious skin and dry it out. In a rare reversal, she was wearing more clothing than Jessica—which was easy, given that Jessica was only wearing a bikini.

Cheeky's attire consisted of a knee-length skirt and a tight white shirt with, 'Man's Best Friends' written across her breasts.

If there was one constant in the universe, it was Cheeky's firm disbelief that shame was an unnecessary evolutionary trait. The pilot sometimes joked she'd had it genetically removed.

"Oh! Check these out!" Cheeky said, holding up what looked like a star that had been cut in half.

"I don't get it," Jessica frowned. "What are those?"

"Not sure…oh! I know," Cheeky laughed and placed them on Jessica's chest. "Star boobs!"

Jessica laughed as the half-stars lit up with a holographic display of solar flares and coronal mass ejections.

"Those are soup bowls," the store owner said as he walked past, carrying something to the front of the curiosity shop.

"You sure?" Cheeky asked. "I bet you'd sell a lot more if you marketed them as protective boob covers."

Jessica snorted and handed the half stars back to Cheeky who continued down the aisle.

<He's going to have to disinfect half his shop before you two are done,> Iris commented.

"We're just putting some extra mystery in the curiosity shop," Cheeky countered.

<*Is* ***that*** *what you call it?*> Iris asked, sending a smirk into their minds.

A laugh burst from Jessica's throat and Cheeky giggled, rolling with the double entendre. "No, but I really should. I bet Finaeus would love to see what's in there."

"Sometimes I can't believe that you two are still together." Jessica said as she picked up an object that was either a pleasure device, or some sort of mixer. Or maybe both. "I expected you to flame out in some amazing explosion long ago."

Cheeky shrugged and walked further down the aisle. "You know how it is, you meet the right guy and things just click."

"I have this distinct memory of you telling me that being monogamous is the same thing as being celibate," Jessica countered.

"Jessica!" Cheeky turned, a wounded expression on her face. "I am *not* monogamous. You take that back! I have a reputation to uphold. Seriously, that's just mean!"

"Yeah, but you haven't been having escapades at any recent stops. If you had you'd've told me. You can't help describing the local flavors."

Cheeky rolled her eyes and picked up a pair of mirrored glasses from the shelf. "We've just had a lot of brief stops. You know I don't like to go far from the ship either."

"Sure thing, Cheeks," Jessica replied.

"Don't make me douse you with pheromones," Cheeky warned with a wink as she put the glasses on. "What do you think of these? Weird, right? How backward is this place if they need glasses for eye protection."

"You know, they look really good on you," Jessica said. "Fluff your hair out, it got all matted from that weird bubble hat."

Cheeky complied, and posed for Jessica. "Hot enough for you to fuck?"

"Cheeky, you've always been hot enough for me to fuck. Timing just never worked out. And now we're both celibate."

"Monogamous," Cheeky replied, pulling down her glasses and winking at Jessica.

"You should buy those," Jessica said.

Cheeky walked to a mirror and looked herself over. "You know, I think I will. I rock this look."

Jessica laughed. "You rock every look. You pay, I'm going to wait outside, I need to bathe in more of the delicious starlight they have here."

"Just don't walk out into traffic or anything," Cheeky warned.

"That was just one time, years ago."

Cheeky's only response was a laugh, and Jessica walked out of the small shop and into Sullus's noon blaze. The moment it struck her skin, she felt a surge of energy flood through her body, a delicious tingle of power and vitality.

"Oh, stars," she moaned as her skin began to glow brightly.

A few passersby glanced at her, some stopping to stare as Jessica walked to the edge of the sidewalk so she wasn't standing in the middle of the foot traffic.

<You've gathered quite the audience,> Iris said as Jessica closed her eyes, turning slowly so every inch of her body took in the life-giving light.

<Don't care,> Jessica said. *<Best part of coming planetside is daylight. It's different with an atmosphere. I don't know how to describe it.>*

<Well, the microbes in your skin were designed to work best with light filtered through an atmosphere. Probably has something to do with their reaction,> Iris supplied.

<Makes sense. Not that I care why it feels so good, I just want to soak it up.>

Jessica continued to slowly turn, basking in the light when suddenly half the free nano drifting around her suddenly shut down, killed off in an EM wave that passed down the street.

Jessica opened her eyes to see a dozen people standing on the sidewalk gazing at her.

"Did you pick that up?" she asked, looking them over.

"Why do you glow?" a woman asked.

"Preference," Jessica replied quickly. "There was an EM pulse, did any of you pick it up?"

Heads wagged, and Jessica frowned. Of course. None of these people would have had any probes out, nano or micro. The EM wave hadn't been strong enough to affect any tech inside their bodies, so there was no way the locals would have noticed.

<Cheeky, did you pick that up?> Jessica asked. *<An EMP went off somewhere nearby.>*

No response came over the Link and Jessica pushed past the crowd into the curiosity shop.

"Cheeky!" she called out, looking down the aisles as she rushed to the sales counter where the proprietor was slowly rising, rubbing his head.

"What the hell?" he muttered.

"Cheeky? Where did she go?" Jessica asked the man.

"What? Who?" he asked clearly confused.

Jessica grabbed shirt collar, locking his eyes on to hers. "The blond woman who was with me. Where is she?"

"She was paying for the glasses…then there was a flash and you were rushing in."

Jessica looked down and stared at the glasses sitting beside a credit chit.

"Shit!" she swore. "You have a back door?"

"Yeah, it's in the back…. What's going on?"

Jessica rushed down the aisles toward the rear of the store, not bothering to answer the man as she reached out to the team.

<Everyone! We have a problem.>

* * * * *

"Do you have any grass-fed beef?" Finaeus asked the woman at the deli counter. "You know, like only grass?"

"I'm sorry, what?" the tall orange-haired woman asked. "You want beef that was grown off grass? Like vat stuff?"

"What? No. I mean beef from cows that only ate grass. Too many places feed cows all sorts of stuff—including other cows. I just want to make sure we get the good stuff. Certified."

The woman—Betty according to her name tag—shook her head. "That sounds like crazy talk. No one on Ferra would do that. We have a billion hectares of grass out there. Why would we feed our cattle anything else?"

A grin split Finaeus' face. "Betty, you're my kinda woman, singing my tune, as it were."

"Uh, sure...you going to place an order? You're holding up the line."

"Yeah, of course, sorry, just reveling in the fact that I'm having this exchange with a human, not a machine."

"Why would you talk to a machine about meat?" Betty asked. "They don't eat meat, they shouldn't sell meat."

"Betty, if I wasn't already with the most beautiful woman in the universe, I'd take you right here. Now, for my order, I need ten round roasts, thirty-two ribeye steaks—make sure they're tender—ten kilos of bone-in short ribs, twenty of your Ferra strip cuts, four turkeys, and thirty-two whole chickens."

Betty shook her head as she noted the items on her holodisplay. "For someone uncertain about whether or not machines eat meat, you certainly know your cuts. Gonna take about twenty minutes to package all that up. You're order number 321."

"Three twenty-one. Got it," Finaeus said and moved out of the way for the next person in line to advise the carnivorous Betty of their desires.

"Fin, check this out," Misha said from the far side of a large cooler filled with fish. "These fish have two tails."

Finaeus peered into the cooler and shook his head. "I guess the *In Future Light* terraformed this world. They always did like making agrarian biomes."

"How does agrarian biomes tie into two-tailed fish?" Misha asked.

"Well, first off, that's not a two-tailed fish, that's a one-headed fishes."

Misha shook his head. "I can never tell if you're messing with me when you say things like that, Finaeus."

"And you'll never be able to, either. But in this case I'm not. The *In Future Light,* didn't have much in the way of ocean life specialists, but they did have ol' Scorry. That man loved to tweak things just so. Every world he ever did had a species of one-headed fishes."

"Why?" Misha asked.

Finaeus shrugged. "Beats the hell out of me. I never got to ask him."

"You terraformers were one strange breed," Misha said with a grin as he pulled several of the fish out of the cooler and wrapped them in a film before putting them in his cart.

"Well yeah, normal people don't decide to become homeless home-builders for the rest of their lives. We were always weirdos."

Once finished in the deli area, Finaeus and Misha split up, each covering half the large market building, gathering the supplies they needed into the carts floating behind them.

It wasn't every stop that they got to hand-select their food, and even less often that they got to do it planet-side where the food was grown.

Ferra was a rare pleasure.

They had a full week down on the dirt while they waited for their outbound shipment to be completed and delivered. More than enough time to really enjoy the local cuisine and culture.

The world of Ferra was what Finaeus liked to call mid-tech, the most common kind in Orion Freedom Alliance space. They were agrarian, largely self-sustaining, but they didn't possess advanced nano or technology that would make them a post-scarcity society.

That meant food and energy were their two main concerns, which—to his mind—gave their culture a certain flavor that translated into their food.

Post scarcity civilizations tended toward bland. They believed they'd solved everything and ceased challenging themselves. It was no surprise to him that the state of a civilization was most evident in their food.

Or you just like food too much, old man.

Finaeus was sometimes amused by his fascination with eating. Thousands of years of living, and a good meal was still one of his favorite things. Maybe it was because he could always count on a delicious new dish to excite him—even though he'd probably already eaten some variation of it on the far side of human space—or an old favorite that brought back fond memories.

Stars, that was half the fun, trying to find the similarities that caused people with nothing else in common to make the same foods.

Though his young companion didn't have the breadth of experience, Misha had the same appreciation for a great spread. Over the last nine years, Finaeus had managed to craft the man into a half-decent cook.

<Fin,> Misha called over the Link, disrupting Finaeus's thoughts about…Misha.

<What?> Finaeus grunted.

<Get some of those melons by the deli, I think I have an idea for a breakfast treat.>

<Sure,> Finaeus walked back toward the fresh produce section which was just beyond the deli.

"Serving 321!" a voice called out, and Finaeus smiled.

"Perfect timing."

He turned toward the deli counter just as a call came into his mind from Jessica.

<Everyone! We have a problem.>

<Define problem,> Finaeus replied. *<I'm just about to pick up the meat order.>*

<It's Cheeky. She's been kidnapped.>

THE MISSING

STELLAR DATE: 03.10.8948 (Adjusted Years)
LOCATION: Outskirts of Parda City, Ferra, Sullus System
REGION: Midway Cluster, Orion Freedom Alliance Space

There had been no sign of Cheeky in the alley running behind the buildings and when Jessica came back in to check on the store owner and ask him if he recalled anything more, a police officer had been waiting.

"Oh, I'm sure she's just off having a good time," Jessica said to the police officer for the third time. "She's a party girl, and if someone said there was a party going on, she'd follow in a heartbeat."

Jessica was losing precious minutes talking to the man, but running off would just raise the wrong type of suspicion and hamper her own search for Cheeky and Piya.

"It's the middle of the day," Dan, the Parda City officer replied. "What sort of party could be going on right now?"

"Oh, who knows," Jessica shrugged. "It could be a mediocre game of snark in a seedy bar. She's not picky. I'm sure she'll turn up soon."

Jessica stood just inside the curiosity shop, glad to be out of the sun and not glowing—as much—for a change. It was one thing to bask in it for fun. It was another to draw a crowd of onlookers while on the lookout for an enemy.

<*We're wasting valuable time,*> Iris said impatiently.

<I know, I know. He's driving me nuts, but I can't just walk off.>

<Every minute Cheeky and Piya are getting further and further away, Jess.>

Jessica knew that all too well. The thought also begged the question, who could even take those two down on this backwater world? The EMP hadn't been strong enough to fry any of Cheeky's internal mods, and the woman was a scrappy fighter—plus she had a pulse pistol strapped to her thigh. If there'd been a struggle, the shop would have evidence of it.

But it was as though she'd never even been there.

"What about you?" the cop asked, looking Jessica up and down. "You a party girl too?"

"Nope," Jessica shook her head. "Happily married. My party days are long behind me."

Dan raised an eyebrow as she took in her soft glow. "So what's with the getup?"

"What getup?" Jessica asked.

"The purple, the glowing, walking around your underwear in the middle of the city—"

"It's a bathing suit."

"There's no beach anywhere near here. And that doesn't answer why you glow."

"Well, firstly," Jessica replied. "Where I come from everyone is purple, and we all glow."

"Oh yeah?" Dan asked. "Where's that?"

"Athabasca."

"Never heard of it."

Jessica shrugged. "There's a lot of stars out there, it's out past the Orion Nebula, in the arm, near the border."

"Really?" Dan asked, his eyes widening. "You're from near the border with the Transcend? I hear they don't follow purity out there."

"Yeah, it's a lot more lax." Jessica nodded. "I can't help how I was born, things are just different near the border. But either way, my friend will be fine. You can check in with me in a day if you want. We're on the—"

"*Verdant Stamen,*" Dan completed the sentence for her. "It came up when I scanned you."

"Great!" Jessica exclaimed and placed a hand on his shoulder, giving him her warmest smile. "And I know how to reach out to you too, just in case she doesn't show."

"OK," Dan said. "I guess there's no evidence of any wrongdoing there. I pulled the feeds, *she* certainly wasn't hiding an EMP anywhere, so whoever set that off was elsewhere."

"Right," Jessica nodded. "Just a weird coincidence."

Dan shrugged. "Yeah, sure."

Jessica knew where he was coming from. Any cop worth his salt wouldn't buy a coincidence like that. The word alone would give him hives. Still, with no evidence to go on, and Cheeky only being 'missing' for twenty minutes, he had no other option than to wait.

"OK, you're free to go," Dan said, and waved Jessica off.

<*Thank stars!*> Iris exclaimed.

"Thanks, Dan." She walked out of the shop and spotted Trevor and Cargo across the street. She waited for a break in the hovercar traffic and then crossed to meet them.

"Where's Nance?" she asked the men as she approached.

"In the shop," Cargo jerked his head to the bakery behind them, "thought it might look weird if we all clustered around waiting for you."

"So what's going on?" Trevor asked. "Cop give you any trouble?"

Jessica turned to look down the long boulevard and its multitude of shops, wondering where Cheeky's abductor—and Cheeky, of course—could be by now. "No…just the usual. But I imagine if I don't let him know that we found her before long, he'll become more curious."

Cargo snorted. "Or he'll just stick it in his backlog and forget about it."

"Not sure about that," Jessica replied, moving into the building's shade. "He seemed to genuinely care."

<*We're back at the ship,*> Finaeus said. <*What do you need?*>

Jessica put a hand to her forehead. <*What? Why are you back at the ship?*>

<*They brought a lot of food,*> Sabrina said, her tone decidedly irate. <*My Cheeky and Piya are lost, and you two are thinking with your stomachs.*>

<*Give me some credit. I care about Cheeky as much as any of you,*> Finaeus replied. <*Misha and I figured that if we all showed up loitering on that street, it would be bad for any amount of subterfuge. Let whoever is watching us wonder what's going on. Try to figure out why we'd just take our food order back to the ship.*>

<*Watching us?*> Cargo asked.

<Yeah, if they hit Cheeky in the five minutes Jessica was sun-worshiping with something that could take her out that fast, this person—or persons—have been watching us.>

<He's got a good point,> Nance said as she walked out of the bakery, a massive donut in hand. *<This isn't some random snatch and grab.>*

Jessica leaned against Trevor and sighed, trying to fight off an impending sense of panic. *<The only thing I could determine was that an EMP was used, and that it was targeted. Really focused.>*

<Sounds like the sort of tech that wouldn't be common on a world like this,> Trevor said.

Nance took a bite of her donut and nodded slowly. *<Sure, but you know that any ship passing through the Sullus System could be anything from an ore hauler to a corporate research vessel. We've seen plenty of places that are little more than nomadic tribes, but they import some of the best tech around.>*

<So here's the thing,> Jessica said. *<We need to figure out the 'why'. Why would someone grab Cheeky?>*

<Sex?> Cargo asked.

<Uninspired, but possible,> Jessica replied. *<What else?>*

<They need a pilot, a getaway driver,> Misha suggested.

<We can't discount RHY Dynamics,> Iris said. *<We spotted one of their research vessels six systems back. What if they followed us?>*

<Why grab Cheeky, though?> Jessica asked. *<I'd be RHY's target, not her.>*

Trevor reached down and stroked Jessica's arm. *<Maybe it was because you were outside doing your*

impression of a flower with a crowd gathered 'round, so they decided to take second best.>

<Kinda tips their hand,> Erin said. *<Better to hold back and wait for Jessica to be alone again.>*

Jessica agreed with Erin's assessment. *<OK, then who have we pissed off enough to chase us and abduct Cheeky?>*

<Lately?> Misha chortled.

Jessica nodded. *<We've travelled over three thousand light years in the past nine years. That's more distance than most people ever dream of covering—unless they have jump gates.>*

<OK, so who have we pissed off in the last five hundred light years?> Cargo asked.

<There was that guy back at Philias,> Trevor suggested. *<He thought we'd ripped him off with that fish we delivered.>*

<Really?> Jessica shook her head. *<Think someone would chase us nine months for fish?>*

<They **were** *expensive fish,>* Iris countered. *<Though I can't imagine why…too many tentacles.>*

Misha made a gagging sound over the Link. *<Stars, don't remind me about those thi—>*

<Hey!> Sabrina interrupted. *<There's a ship docked at one of the stations in orbit that we ran into three systems back.>*

<Really?> Cargo asked. *<In…Hallas? Which ship and station?>*

<It was at Sergis Station same time as us. Ship's name is the Laren.>

Sabrina passed the details over the Link, and Jessica looked the ship over. It was a freighter. Not a small one either. The *Laren* measured in at over three kilometers in length, and could haul millions of tons of cargo. It was a bit strange to see a ship like that in a system like Sullus. Unless it planned to pick up *a lot* of beef.

<Doesn't seem like the sort of ship you sneak around in,> Iris said before Jessica could.

<She's right,> Cargo replied. *<Ship like that does not scream stealth.>*

<Do they make regular calls here?> Jessica asked.

Sabrina's mental tone was short. *<Checking. The STC NSAIs here are a real bunch of asshats. Who makes them like that? NSAIs have no personalities. Someone had to* ***program*** *them to be dickheads.>*

<Stuff's weird in the retro-zone,> Cargo replied with a shrug of his shoulders.

The retro-zone was a name the crew had given to the region of space they were currently traveling through. The official name was the Orion-Perseus Expansion Transit District 4A. A fancy way of saying a region of space that lay close to the Inner Stars, and which had to keep its use of advanced technology to a minimum to ensure they remained undetected by Inner Stars civilizations.

Many of the systems within the retro-zone were settled by refugees during the FTL wars; ships that had fled into the far reaches of space, only to meet up with the FGT who had worlds ready for them.

The trade-off, however, was an enforced limitation on technological advances, specifically advanced personal mods and a near-ban on sentient AI.

It was markedly different from the further reaches of Orion Space, which were even more advanced than

Inner Stars civilizations—with no limitations to speak of when it came to advanced mods. As evidenced by what RHY Dynamics had done to Jessica.

The only constant was the dearth of sentient AI.

<I see that some of the Laren's *crew is down here on Ferra. Captain too,>* Cargo said. *<They're staying at a resort by the northern mountains.>*

<Whatever for?> Nance asked. *<There's nothing up there on Ferra.>*

<Skiing,> Erin supplied.

<Pfft,> Nance breathed out derisively and shook her head. *<Seriously? That thing where people strap things to their feet and slide down snowy mountains?>*

Jessica patted Nance on the shoulder. *<Some people like to be cold. It's their jam.>*

<Sounds like madness to me,> Nance replied.

<It's only forty five minutes by maglev,> Cargo said. *<Someone can hop up there, scope them out. See what there is to see.>*

<I nominate Jessica,> Nance said. *<She seems to know all about that stuff.>*

Jessica shook her head and turned back to peer at the curiosity shop across the street. *<No chance. I'm our lead detective. I don't go off to chase down crazy leads.>*

<How'd you get to be lead detective?> Misha asked. *<Is it because you were a super-hero?>*

<No, Mish, it's because I ***was*** *a detective. And I still* ***am*** *a super hero. Retyna Girl never chases down weak leads! She has sidekicks for that.>*

<So who's the sidekick that gets to go freeze their ass off?> Nance asked.

<You should go,> Finaeus said with a grin over the Link. *<Would build character.>*

<I repeat, pfft!>

<I'll go,> Trevor volunteered. *<If those bastards have Cheeky for…well, some reason I can't discern, they're gonna regret it.>*

<I'll join you,> Cargo said to Trevor. *<It's just a short trip, we'll be back by evening.>*

The idea of splitting the team up didn't sit well with Jessica, but a ship like the *Laren* appearing here after being at the same station as them all the way back in Philia *was* unusual. Especially since it wasn't a regular stop for the massive freighter.

She nodded slowly, looking Cargo, then Trevor in the eyes. "You two be careful. A lot of coincidences here."

Cargo nodded solemnly. "Don't worry. If we need an extract, you can fly the pinnace over and give us a hand."

"The pinnace?" Nance asked with a grin. "Do you mean the *Sexy*?"

"No, I mean the pinnace."

<OK. That's settled, the boys are going to go north to the mountains. Nance and I are going to follow some leads here in the city.>

<What leads are those?> Nance asked.

<We're going to look into every single vehicle that left this area in the last twenty minutes. Iris has already worked her way into the local traffic systems.>

<What should we do?> Misha asked.

Nance laughed. *<Make lunch.>*

<I feel like none of you are taking this seriously enough!> Sabrina said, sounding exasperated. *<Cheeky is* ***missing*** *and you're all goofing off.>*

<Sorry, Sabrina,> Jessica said, her tone conciliatory. *<Pesky organic stress responses. I'm not too worried yet, because if it's a local group, they're holding her for ransom, and will contact us soon. If it's someone from offworld, they want something and also won't hurt her yet.>*

<Yet,> Iris repeated.

<Right. Yet. OK, Finaeus, can you help Sabrina review profiles of ships on planet and docked above? The Laren *may not be the only vessel that we've seen before, just the only one using the same name.>*

<You got it. Misha, finish stowing all this food, then meet me on the bridge. We get to match scan and burn profiles!>

<Joy.>

"Let's go," Cargo slapped Trevor on the back. "We've got a maglev to catch."

"And some mountains to fall down."

"What exactly are we doing?" Nance asked Jessica. "We're going to look at every vehicle that left the area? That has to be in the thousands since Cheeky disappeared."

"Close to five thousand, yeah," Jessica said. "But Iris and Erin will be able to go through them faster than us. You and I are going to do the legwork."

"Gonna show all that leg while doing the legwork?" Nance asked, looking Jessica over.

Jessica chuckled. "I don't really blend in here, do I?"

"Jess, you don't blend in most places, but down here, yeah, not even a little bit."

Jessica fingered a lock of her hair. "Ship's thirty minutes out. Looks like I have to go shopping."

A nervous laugh burst from Nance's throat. "Jess, only you could turn Cheeky's abduction into an excuse for a shopping trip."

"It'll just be something simple," Jessica said. "We're not going partying or anything. Cheeky and I passed by a place that looked promising a block back."

Ten minutes later, Jessica and Nance stepped out of the store. Little they carried fit Jessica's exaggerated figure, and in the end she had resorted to buying a long, white and blue dress. She wore a loose white jacket overtop, matched by a broad rimmed white hat.

"You're still glowing a bit," Nance said as they stepped out onto the sidewalk once more.

"I know, my little microbes are fully charged. There's no stopping them when they get like this."

<Get to the alley behind that curiosity shop,> Iris instructed. *<We need your meaty appendages to check something out.>*

<Oh yeah?> Nance asked as the two women began to walk down the street. *<I don't know how much meat Jess has in her fingers. I think they're all poly-skin, carbon fiber, and alien germs.>*

<I'll have you know I still have all my natural muscle. Sort of.>

Nance laughed. *<Sort of.>*

<Well, it's enhanced, but it's still there.>

They reached the alley and Jessica looked up and down the narrow stretch of road. City trash receptacles lined the alley, and little else—Ferra was nothing if not a clean planet.

"So what do you need our fleshy bits for?" Jessica asked.

<*Iris and I have wormed our way into all their local traffic control systems,*> Erin began. <*We have every bit of movement within twenty blocks mapped out. Problem is, no cars or foot traffic left this alley the entire time.*>

<*Cheeky wasn't carried out slung over someone's shoulder,*> Jessica countered. <*People would have noticed that.*>

<*And we'd've seen it on the streets,*> Iris said in agreement.

<*So no cams cover this alley?*> Nance asked.

Erin sent a mental affirmation. <*That's correct. Video coverage here in Parda City is spotty at best.*>

<*So when you said you needed our fleshy digits, what you really meant was that you wanted us to walk over here so you could use my nanocloud to get a local tap into the cameras on the street here to see if the original recording matches the feeds.*>

<*She's a smart one, Iris,*> Erin said with ghost of a smirk in their minds.

<*I'm in,*> Iris said a moment later. <*Annnnd nothing. This camera's local storage agrees with what it transmitted. Go to the far end of the alley, let's see what that camera has to say.*>

Jessica and Nance shared a look and walked down the alley. Iris directed Jess's nanocloud up to the camera mounted on a building and a minute later they were staring at a deepening mystery.

It was confirmed. There was no sign of anyone exiting the alley.

Jessica crouched down beside a drain pipe and wrapped a hand around it, discharging some of her skin's accumulated energy into the ground.

"That helped," Nance said. "You are decidedly less glowy."

"Good," Jessica said as she rose and dusted off her dress. "Getting tired of the gawking."

Over the next ten minutes, Jessica and Nance circled the block, the AIs tapping every camera as the two women spoke with store owners, looking for any clue that someone had come through with a small blonde woman slung over their shoulder.

In the end they were back in the mouth of the alley, no closer to finding the abductor's egress route than before.

"It's like they just flew away," Nance muttered as she looked to the sky.

"Yeah," Jessica said in agreement as she leant against one of the buildings, staring down the alley. "But that would be on the ATC logs. No way to hide that."

"You sure?" Nance asked. "We seem to have a magician on our hands here."

"Magician…" Jessica said as she stared down the alley. Then something clicked. "Nance, you are really, really going to hate this."

"Why?" Nance asked as Jessica began to stride toward the back of the curiosity shop.

Jessica stopped and looked down at a sewer access cover.

"Oh, *hell* no!" Nance said. "You're not getting me down there without a hazsuit. No way, no how. I just bought these boots too!"

"I thought that you don't worry about being fashionable," Jessica said as she crouched and stuck her fingers in the three holes on the cover.

"Not like you and Cheeky, no, but I do like boots that aren't soaked in piss and shit. Call me crazy."

Jessica lifted the cover free and set it aside, sending her nano down into the hole. "Looks like it's just a storm drain, Nance. No piss and shit in there."

Nance snorted. "Not human, no, but guess where the animals go?"

<The nano can scout the tunnels,> Iris offered. *<You don't really need to go down there.>*

"I know," Jessica chuckled. "But messing with Nance was worth it."

"Dammit, Jess!"

<OK, now we're cooking,> Iris said. *<I've got one of Cheeky's hairs down here. This is definitely the abductor's egress route.>*

"Of course, you know what that means, right, Jess?" Nance asked.

Jessica nodded. "They could be anywhere by now."

MOUNTAINS AND GEESE

STELLAR DATE: 03.10.8948 (Adjusted Years)
LOCATION: Nise Maglev Line, Ferra, Sullus System
REGION: Midway Cluster, Orion Freedom Alliance Space

"Feels like a wild goose chase," Trevor said as he settled into his seat on the train. "Why would they abduct Cheeky and then go on a ski trip?"

"Could just be cover," Cargo said. "Ship like that has a big crew, plenty of people to pull off a snatch and grab while the captain and officers take a little vacation."

"You realize that if they're after us, we can't just walk up and start asking them questions. They're gonna know who we are."

Cargo thought about the possibility for a moment. "Subterfuge really isn't our thing, is it?"

"Not even a little bit," Trevor replied. "That's the girls' gig. We're usually just the muscle behind their plays. Well, at least I am."

Cargo caught the implication. Sure, he was *Sabrina*'s captain, and most of the time he directed all the ship's operations, but everyone knew that when push came to shove, Jessica called the shots as often as not.

It didn't bother him, she was a skilled pilot, had captained much larger ships than *Sabrina,* and had been in more fights than anyone he knew.

Most of the time. It didn't bother him most of the time.

<You don't normally let it get to you,> Hank said. *<You and Jessica make a good team leading the ship.>*

<Yeah, and she's very good about not seizing control. I guess I'm just worried about Cheeky and Piya. We've gotten too blasé out here, acting like nothing can hurt us—which is mostly true—but all it takes is a bullet to the head, and they're gone.>

Hank nodded solemnly in Cargo's mind. *<We're not going to let anything happen to them.>*

<And if something does….> Cargo let the thought hang.

Hank let slip a grim laugh. *<I know a starship that can smash planets.>*

"I didn't mean anything by it," Trevor said, correctly interpreting the cause of Cargo's silence.

Cargo laughed. "It's OK. Hank was just telling me not to be such a baby."

<I was a touch more subtle than that.>

"You were, but I'm not," Cargo replied. "I guess that's why the girls do the sneaky stuff, and we go bust heads."

"Except for Finaeus," Trevor added. "That guy's like a ninja. Just appears out of nowhere."

"Must be all those years on the run."

Trevor nodded silently, and Cargo stared out the window wondering how they would feel out the crew of the *Laren*. He pulled up the list of crew Sabrina had located at the ski resort, a place named Killashandra Mountain. The name rang a bell, but he couldn't place it just now.

Sabrina hadn't accessed the resort's member list, just a flight record of a shuttle leaving the *Laren* and landing at Killashandra. The STC records showed the *Laren*'s

Captain—a woman named Hunter—was at the helm of the shuttle, but no other passengers were listed.

That didn't mean she was the only one aboard. A private ship like the *Laren*'s shuttle wouldn't be required to list passengers.

Customs would have the records, and Cargo considered asking Iris to access their systems but decided against it. For now, they'd use some old fashioned legwork to find out who had come down from the ship.

Or, at the least, see if they could access Killashandra Mountain's surveillance feeds.

"So if they were following us," Cargo said after looking over the information he had, "they *will* know who we are. I think we do a frontal approach. Find out where they are and simply show up. Their reactions should tell us everything we need to know."

Trevor chuckled. "Well, depending on where they are. If they're asleep in their rooms the reaction will be startlement whether they're involved with Cheeky or not."

"Sorry, in my mind they were at a bar or something."

"You know, Cargo, not everyone hangs out in bars. Some people do other things with their spare time."

Cargo frowned. "Like what? Gamble?"

"Or read a book, go to a museum, take in a live show somewhere."

"A live show of what? Like acrobats or something?"

"Yeah, or music. Heck, some people even go bowling."

"Trevor, no one goes bowling, that's just some ancient game you see in old vids."

Trevor held up his hands. "OK, you got me. But they could be curling."

"Well yeah, that I could see. Everyone loves to throw a rock from time-to-time."

"So we just need to figure out where they like to hang out—other than on the mountain. I don't think you and I are skiing material."

Cargo nodded in agreement. "I'll see if Iris can help us with surveillance."

"Send in the A—" Trevor stopped himself as Cargo raised his eyebrows. *<Right, sometimes I forget how folk in the retro-zone react to AIs.>*

Cargo shook his head as he reached out to Iris. *<Hey, Iris, you busy?>*

<Cargo, we're working on Piya and Cheeky's abduction, of course I'm busy.>

<Sorry, poor choice of words. What I was curious about was whether or not you can hop into the resort's network and access their surveillance feeds. We want to find out where our quarry likes to hang out.>

<Sure, just—huh…look at that.>

<Look at what?> Cargo asked.

<That resort doesn't have any Link access.>

Cargo wasn't sure if Iris was messing with him or not. *<What do mean, 'no Link access'?>*

<Do I look like some sort of riddle machine, Cargo? I mean they have one hard-wired network connection for managing bookings and taking payment, but that's it. There is no other network there to speak of. Not even any wireless service

towers. Anyone wanting to make a Link connection to the outside world better have a satellite hookup.>

<*Iris?*> Cargo asked in a kindly tone, <*Trevor and I will be in that group of people wanting Link.*>

Iris snorted. <*Cargo, you're a grown man, and I'm not your travel agent. You and Trevor have the hardware for a satellite hookup—provided you're outside. Buy time on a satcomm network and call it a day.*>

<*Yeah, thanks, Iris.*> Cargo closed the connection. <*She seems testy,*> he commented to Hank.

<*Yeah, she and Piya have grown really close over the years. The two of them were planning on melding and producing children.*>

<*Really?*> Cargo was surprised to hear the two AI were considering a meld. Not that he followed the romantic—or whatever they'd be called—interests of the AIs. He barely paid attention to the human ones onboard.

<*Yeah, we don't really talk about that stuff with organics. You ask too many weird questions.*>

Cargo shook his head. *He* certainly wouldn't have.

<*OK,*> Hank continued. <*There's only one satcomm network that covers that part of the planet…which isn't surprising, there are only four satcomm networks at Ferra to begin with. I'm booking time on it for all of us.*>

<*Thanks, Hank,*> Cargo said as he leant back in his seat and gave Trevor a grim look.

"No network up there. Hank's getting us satcomm time."

<*Does that mean no surveillance access?*> Trevor asked the group privately, looking worried about the prospect.

<They may still have it, it'll just be on an offline network.> Hank replied.

<So if we have to hack it, we'll be on our own,> Cargo confirmed. *<I wouldn't want to route Iris through one of us on a low-band Link to do that. Would probably flag something with the satcomm company.>*

<Well, given the luddites we're dealing with, I can probably walk onto their network anyway,> Hank said. *<Or whatever they're running up there.>*

Cargo nodded, and they rode the rest of the way to Killashandra Mountain in silence, each wondering what they were going to encounter, and whether or not it would be worth the time it took to get out to the resort.

* * * * *

The train made its final stop in a quaint town named Spyglass and the two men exited the maglev car and looked up at the towering peaks around them.

"These are some damn tall mountains," Trevor said, moving aside to clear the way for other passengers. "They have to be at least four kilometers above us."

"All the better to ski down," a man said with a wink as he walked past.

"Sure is beautiful down here, too," Trevor said with an appreciative smile as he looked around at the snow-covered town.

"It's freakin' freezing is what it is," Cargo muttered and wrapped his arms around himself. "Can you believe that people actually *live* here? Of their own free will?"

Trevor laughed and slapped Cargo on the back. "You got some meat on you, should be enough to keep you warm."

Cargo snorted. "Trevor, you have the metabolism of this entire town combined. Of course, *you're* not cold."

"It's just a five-klick walk out to the resort, if we jog it'll keep us warm."

"And what if we have to go hunting for them all over a mountain?" Cargo asked.

Trevor sighed. "You're such a baby. I see a store across the plaza there that looks like they sell cold-weather gear. Let's go see what they have to offer."

The store turned out to specialize in all sorts of winter gear, unsurprisingly focused on skiing. They had everything from puffy, down-filled coats to three-millimeter-thick skinsuits rated to keep a person warm clear down to minus eighty degrees.

Cargo grabbed one of those, a large jacket, a long scarf and a thick woolen hat.

"You're gonna boil," Trevor said as he tried on his seventh jacket. Even the store's largest size couldn't make it around his shoulders.

"I'd rather boil than freeze," Cargo grunted as he walked to the front of the store to pay at the counter. The woman working the checkout quickly scanned the items and gave him a warm smile.

"You must have been cold out there, its minus-thirty today."

Cargo nodded. "Tell me about it. Coming up here was a spur of the moment decision. We're gonna throw ourselves down the mountain and see what happens."

The woman laughed and fingered a lock of her black hair while looking Cargo over. "You're not…modded to look like that, are you?"

"To look like what?" Cargo asked.

"Your skin, it's so dark, but it looks creamy too. I've never seen anyone with skin like that. Folks down south are kinda red, but no one is like you. You're almost black!"

<*These people need to travel more,*> Cargo said privately to Hank.

<*Kid's young, barely even twenty-five,*> Hank replied. <*Can you blame her?*>

<*I'd been to three hundred and twenty-five star systems by the time I was her age.*>

Hank chuckled softly in Cargo's mind. <*Yeah, but you were found amongst a bunch of shipping crates when you were two. Hardly the same circumstances.*>

The woman was starting to look embarrassed by Cargo's silence, and he gave her a tired smile. "Totally natural. You must have heard of what happens if your ancestors stay in a place that gets a lot of sunlight for a few thousand years. Non-adaptive melanin."

"Oh, I know," the girl said with a vigorous nod. Then she leaned forward and whispered. "Is it true what else they say?"

Hank burst out laughing in his mind, and Cargo was glad his blush was hard to see. A half-dozen responses flowed through his mind before he finally sputtered. "Girl, I'm old enough to be your great grandfather."

"So was my last boyfriend," the girl said with a wink. "I like older men, they've got the right kind of *experience*."

"Uh, yeah, lots of that, enough to know when to keep our pants on."

"Yeah, but you have to take them off anyway," the woman continued unabashed. "I mean, you bought that nice, tight skinsuit to keep you warm. It won't fit over what you're wearing. Why don't you go into one of the changing rooms and put it on while you're here?"

Hank was still laughing in Cargo's mind, which wasn't helping his concentration much. Despite the fact that the woman wanted to check out his equipment, she *was* right. He did buy the warm clothes to wear. Changing here would be ideal. It would also get him away from the clerk.

"Yeah, good idea," Cargo said with a smile and walked back toward the changing rooms.

Once inside he locked the door and quickly stripped down before pulling on the skinsuit. The chill that had set into him during the brief time outside was instantly forgotten as the suit's warmth embraced him.

"Damn, that feels a lot better."

The door rattled, and suddenly opened, the woman from the front counter standing before him.

"Uh…that was locked," Cargo said.

"I have the codes," she replied with a wink and stepped toward him, her eyes trailing down his body and stopping on the bulge at his crotch.

A smile grew on her lips and she asked, "Is that natural too? No mods? I don't like mods."

"Yeah, of course," Cargo said as he took a step back biting his cheek as he stared down at the lithe woman before him.

<Trevor, you find a jacket yet?> Cargo asked.

<Almost, the clerk thinks he has one that will fit, he just has to find it. I booked us a ride up to the resort. It'll be here in ten minutes.>

Ten minutes…

"Good," the woman said with a lascivious grin as she took another step forward, her breasts brushing against Cargo's chest. "I like to do things one hundred percent natural."

Ten minutes later, Cargo and Trevor stood outside waiting for the car that would take them to the resort.

"Hey Cargo," Trevor said as he leaned over.

"Yeah?" Cargo asked, feeling too warm in the skinsuit, his clothes, the jacket, scarf and hat. He wasn't sure if the clothing—or the events preceding getting dressed—was to blame.

"You've uhhh, got something on your face."

"Where?" Cargo asked quickly.

Trevor chuckled. "Left cheek, a bit more rouge then you normally wear."

Cargo wiped at his cheek. "Says the man in the pink jacket with blue flowers."

Trevor looked down at his jacket and grinned. "Not every man can rock pink with flowers. But an elite few can. I am one of those few."

It was Cargo's turn to laugh. "You really believe that?"

"Cargo, seriously. I hooked up with the hottest woman in the galaxy on the first night I met her."

"Really?" Cargo asked. "You and Jessica? That first night?"

"What? No! She was beaten to a bloody pulp. I mean we were an item that first night. Even before the cage match. It's why what's-her-name pulled a fast one on Jessica in the first place."

"'What's-her-name'?"

"Yeah, I've forgotten it. She shall never be named again."

"I've got a few of those in my past too," Cargo replied with a nod.

The men stood in silence for a minute before Trevor leaned in close again

"There's still a bit there on your cheek."

"The flowers look stupid."

* * * * *

Cargo had to admit he was impressed by the Killashandra Mountain resort. The main building was massive, constructed from stone with towering wooden pillars supporting the roof.

The overall look was one of a hunting lodge from ancient stories—if that hunting lodge had been built by giants.

The car let them out at the resort's front doors, and the two men stood on the curb considering their next move.

<I saw a shuttle come down while we were on approach,> Trevor said. *<Looks like the landing pad is a couple of klicks to the east, over that ridge.>*

Cargo nodded absently. *<I did as well. Let's see if we can find anything before we hike out there.>*

<I don't see any surveillance cameras,> Hank added. *<Either there aren't any, or they're so small I can't pick them up.>*

<Ferra has almost no crime, especially up here,> Cargo said. *<Other than the maglev platform, there wasn't any monitoring down in the town, either.>*

"Let's check out the bar, first," Cargo said aloud. "Why jump through all these hoops to figure out where they'll be if they're just having a drink."

Trevor shrugged. "Sure, I could use a drink anyway." Then he asked privately, *<What if we see them.>*

<Like I said before. We walk past and see how they react.>

<Or you could have sex with their captain,> Trevor said with a wide grin.

<Shut up, Trevor.>

A SHIP BY ANY OTHER NAME

STELLAR DATE: 03.10.8948 (Adjusted Years)
LOCATION: Parda City Spaceport, Ferra, Sullus System
REGION: Midway Cluster, Orion Freedom Alliance Space

"Stars, this is miserable," Misha complained as he looked over another series of flagged ship builds, and matched them against the vessels from the last seven ports.

<*It's worse with you complaining about it every five minutes,*> Sabrina said tersely.

"No, I think it's just as bad either way," Misha countered. "You're a freaking AI, a damn smart one too. How can *I* help?"

<*You can tell the difference between cyan peppers grown in different regions of the same planet,*> Sabrina said, her mental tone moderated, but still colored with annoyance. <*You have excellent differentiating skills. You just need to apply them to things other than taste.*>

"You're still way faster at this than I am," Misha muttered as he compared one of the ships currently at the space port with other vessels of similar builds they'd encountered in the past.

"We're all double checking each other's work," Finaeus said from his console. "And I'm feeding every one we flag through a more detailed pattern-matching system. We have to look at them from every angle."

Misha nodded silently and went through another batch, ruling out ships that could never be disguised as any of the ships currently on, or around Ferra.

"I'm going to stretch my legs," Misha said as he rose. "Starting to cramp up—don't worry," he added quickly. "I'll still do 'em in my head."

Finaeus nodded and Sabrina sent a mental acknowledgement as Misha walked off the bridge, slowly moving aft toward the lounge on the ship's upper deck, a nice glass of brandy his goal.

The door slid aside and he was surprised to see that afternoon had turned to dusk. They'd been at this longer than he'd realized.

Ferra's larger moon, Ur, hung low over the horizon, and Misha wondered why it was such a strange color of blue. He shrugged the question off and walked to the liquor cabinet where he pulled out his favorite brandy. It was a label they'd shipped a year ago, but one crate had never been delivered due to 'breakage'.

Courtesy of his ocular implants, another set of ships appeared in front of him to examine, and he flipped through them with eye gestures while pouring his drink.

"Stars, so many damn ships," he muttered as he took a sip and then sat on one of the seats, looking out the window.

A batch of local shuttles were next, and he flipped through them quickly. They were just insystem transports, but then he looked past them to the moon and an idea came to mind.

Misha pulled up all the schedules of all the ships running shuttles from Ferra to Ur, cross-referencing them with the STC's arrival time logs.

One stood out. A shuttle run by a company called Peerless Transport had arrived an hour early on its last flight down from Ur. That had been at 0912 this very morning.

Misha checked the current status of the ship. It was still on Ferra. Not at Parda City's spaceport, but at a spaceport five hundred kilometers to the west; one not listed as the shuttle's normal destination.

His curiosity was piqued. Peerless Transport's information feed listed the shuttle's flight from the moon as cancelled, but there it was, resting not far away on the planet's surface.

He pulled up the public logs of ships docked on Ur. Neither of them had reviewed vessels on the moons yet, but something about this stood out to him. Sure, there were a thousand legitimate reasons why the shuttle could be down on the planet. Anything from needing a cheaper planet-side repair, to the CEO needing a ride for a meeting.

But if Misha were looking to get onto Ferra—while still having a reliable, non-public way off—that's just the sort of thing he'd consider.

Then he looked at all ships that had landed in the last two days at Yessen, the city on the moon from where the shuttle had departed.

A minute later, he was back on the bridge, tossing the visual and specs of a ship on the main holo. "Sabina, Fin, check this ship out."

"Where's that ship docked?" Finaeus asked. "Doesn't look like any in our queues.

"It's on Ur, the moon."

<Misha, what are you—>

"Just look at the ship. It matches one we saw four systems ago, back in Mercer."

"OK…it's close," Finaeus agreed. "That ship was the *Flying Srian*, and this one is the *Sierra Echo*."

<*Hull's a close match, though we never really saw the* Flying Srian, *it was docked half-way across the system when we were in Mercer.*>

"See, Finaeus, not wasting time," Misha said with a smug smile.

"You were the one whining that it was a waste of time," Finaeus said with a sigh. "Don't exp—shit!"

<*What is it?*> Sabrina asked, her mental tone rising in pitch. <*What did you find?*>

Finaeus was concentrating on his display and waved a hand behind him. "Just give me a sec, kay?"

Misha stood silently while Sabrina made a soft ticking sound over the bridge's audible systems.

"Dammit, Sabs, can you stop making that sound?" Finaeus asked irritably.

<*Oh, sorry, didn't mean to transmit that.*>

Finaeus stood and turned to Misha. "Well shit, Misha. You just found us a BOGSY."

"A Bogsy?" Misha asked with a frown.

"Bad Orion Guard Ship."

<*What does the Y stand for?*> Sabrina asked.

Finaeus shrugged. "Just seemed better with a Y."

"So it's an Orion Guard ship?" Misha was perplexed. "We're in Orion space, that's not a surprise."

<*True, but the Orion Guard does not heavily patrol the retro-zone. We've only seen a dozen OG cruisers ships in the last year.*>

A second ship appeared on the main display. "Notice any similarities?" Finaeus asked.

<They look like the same class,> Sabrina said. *<Not **exactly** the same, this one looks like it has larger engines and more fuel capacity.>*

"The ship I put up is one of Orion's new stealth scouts. Well, it was new forty years ago," Finaeus said as he leaned against his console. "They were using those ships for their Inner Stars infiltration work."

"The BOGAs," Misha confirmed, remembering the name Finaeus used for the Orion Guard's spy organization.

"One and the same," Finaeus replied.

<But what's a BOGA ship doing here,> Sabrina said. *<I thought they operated outside Orion's borders, just like The Hand.>*

Finaeus shrugged. "That's the only place The Hand ever ran into them. But Kirkland also has internal police forces too. Some public, some secret."

"I've heard of one of those," Misha said. "Out on the far side of Stillwater. We called them the Widows."

"Really?" Finaeus asked. "Why's that?"

"I've only heard rumors, but they were the ones the Feds would send in if someone was trafficking in illegal tech. The stories always have them clothed in black, always women. They'd appear, seize the tech, often killing whoever had it, and then be gone like that," Misha said, snapping his fingers for emphasis.

<So you knew someone, who knew someone?> Sabrina asked.

"Close. I knew a guy who saw one, once. He was going to do a deal for some genetic mods. The life extending ones."

Finaeus crossed his arms. "So how'd your friend escape."

"Well, he didn't trust the seller, so he was scouting the place out. It was going down in a section of a station that was cordoned off for repairs. He sent in some probes and was watching remote feeds when he spotted a shadow that moved."

<*Shadows move all the time,*> Sabrina interjected.

"Hey, let me tell this," Misha replied. "Anyway, he watched the shadow as it slipped through the station, until it got to the meeting place. He kept trying to see what was casting it, but he couldn't. It didn't look like a person, more like an amorphous blob. Anyway, when it got to the meeting place, it stopped moving. Before long the seller showed up. That's when the shadow suddenly formed into a woman."

Misha took a sip of the bourbon he'd brought in with him before continuing. "She was sheathed in black. Her head, face, everything. The seller guy, well, he freaked. I guess he'd heard the rumors as well. He tried to run, but then black tendrils shot out from the Widow's hands and caught his neck."

"Tendrils?" Finaeus asked. "Solid, or particulate?"

Misha shrugged. "I forgot to ask. Either way the tendrils killed the guy fast. A lot quicker than choking. He said the Widow took the case with the tech, wrapped it in something, and then she and the case turned back into a shadow and left."

"Sounds like personal stealth tech," Finaeus mused. "Your friend's probes probably picked up some EM shadow or something caused by the stealth system. They're good, but not perfect."

Misha then explained how the Peerless Transport shuttle from Ur had been cancelled, but still made the trip down to Ferra.

<*So do you think that one of these Widows has Cheeky?*> Sabrina asked. <*What would they want with her?*>

"If they're a secret government agency, they'll have much better tech than the Orion populace gets their hands on," Finaeus replied. "Maybe one of us screwed up, tipped our hand, and they investigated."

<*So you think this BOGSY Widow has been chasing us for four systems?*>

Finaeus ran a hand through his hair and walked across the bridge, then turned and walked back. "I don't know what to think. We're off in pure speculation-land right now. All we *do* know is that a very uncommon Orion Guard vessel is currently docked up on Ur, and its linked to a shuttle that came down at an unusual time to an unusual place."

<*That's more than a little coincidence,*> Sabrina said.

Misha stared at the ship on the holo, remembering how creeped out his friend had been when telling the story of the Widow. "We need to call the girls."

<*Already on it,*> Sabrina replied.

PEERLESS TRANSPORT

STELLAR DATE: 03.10.8948 (Adjusted Years)
LOCATION: Parda City, Ferra, Sullus System
REGION: Midway Cluster, Orion Freedom Alliance Space

"The *fuck*!" Jessica swore and slammed her fist into the stairwell door. "We've checked fifty exits from the storm drainage system and there's not a single sign of them anywhere!"

<Easy, Jess, we'll find them,> Iris said, her soothing tone coming across as forced.

Nance leant against the wall and tugged at the thick braid into which her long brown hair was woven. "They had to leave the tunnels somewhere."

"And we've checked fifty exits out of thousands," Jessica replied. "We could spend a year doing this and never turn up a trace."

<This isn't like you, Jessica,> Iris said. *<You can't give up.>*

"I just figured whoever had taken Cheeky would be an amateur, that they'd leave a trail. But this was a pro, and the trail's getting cold, fast."

"We could split up," Nance offered. "We'll cover more ground like that. I know you think it's too risky, but—"

"But it's too risky," Jessica countered. "We're dealing with someone who was able to snatch Cheeky right out from under my nose. If we go off on our own we'll just add to the missing."

<*Hey, you guys found anything yet?*> Sabrina said broke into their conversation, a strange note in her voice.

<*We've found that we can't find whoever this is,*> Jessica retorted. <*Any luck on your end?*>

<*Yeah, Misha found a clue. We located a ship on Ur—*>

<*The moon?*> Nance interrupted.

<*Yeah, Ur, the moon. We were in the same system as this other ship a couple months ago. But that's not the half of it.*>

<*Do go on,*> Jessica prompted.

Sabrina proceeded to explain the ship's Orion connections, and related Misha's story of the Widows—which would explain how Cheeky's abductor was able to disappear so completely. Though the Orion Guard using an all-female group of assassin tech hunters struck her as hard to believe.

Jessica started up the stairwell. <*I think we should take the* Sexy *and check out the shuttle that came from Ur. There may be clues, and it's obviously this person's planned escape route.*>

<*If we're going up against some Orion secret agent person, we're going to need to gear up,*> Nance said. <*We can't just show up and demand Cheeky back.*>

<*I'll get the* Sexy *ready,*> Sabrina said. <*Actually, I can send it to pick you up if you want me to. There's a transport pad near you where I can set it down.*>

<*Perfect,*> Jessica replied as she and Nance reached the parking garage's main floor. <*Send us the location and we'll meet it there, then we'll boot on out to that spaceport and see what's the deal with our mystery shuttle.*>

<*On it,*> Sabrina replied.

"I don't like it," Nance said as they walked out of the building to the sidewalk. "I feel like we're leaving Cheeky and Piya behind. They're probably still in the city, you know."

<*Iris and I have a line into the police and emergency networks,*> Erin said. <*We'll know if anything comes up. Finaeus and Misha are still on hand if she turns up in the city.*>

"Pardon me if I'm not super-excited about the two of them riding to the rescue," Nance muttered.

"Calling a car," Jessica said. "Misha's come a long way, I've been working with him a lot. Finaeus is no slouch either."

"OK, sure," Nance replied. "Still rather it be us who find her."

Jessica nodded. "I hear you there. You never know. Maybe we'll catch up with the mysterious Widow out at this other spaceport."

"Jess, you don't really believe that, do you?" Nance asked as a car drew up to the curb and Jessica pulled open the door.

Jessica gestured for Nance to get in first. "Yes and no. Stealth tech like Misha described was not uncommon back in Sol. That the Orion Guard would have it at their disposal does not surprise me. An all-female black-ops team? I suppose it's possible, but it seems odd to leave men out. What purpose could that serve?"

Nance shrugged as Jessica closed the door. "Well, if it is one of those Widows who has Cheeky, we'll have to ask her. After we beat the shit out of her, at least."

<Wouldn't you want to beat someone right to the point **before** *the shit comes out?>* Erin asked. *<Shit doesn't really bother me that much, but you two have a definite aversion to it.>*

Nance placed her hand on her face. "Trying to add some levity to the situation, Erin?"

<A bit. Does it help?>

Jessica chuckled. "I'm all in favor of lightening the mood—no pun intended—but poop jokes rarely work for that."

<Trevor and Cargo like them. Finaeus is a master of the poop joke,> Erin countered.

"Then leave it to the masters," Nance replied.

Seven minutes later the car pulled up at the public transport pad. The pad wasn't much more than a large lot behind a shopping district where light shuttles, and VTOL aircraft could touch down.

"There she is." Jessica pointed into the deepening dusk at the gleaming shape of the SS *Sexy* lowering onto the pad.

<Your chariot has arrived,> Sabrina said. *<It occurred to me, though. If this Orion agent knows about us, they probably know about the* Sexy *too. How're you going to fly to that other space port without alerting them?>*

<We're not flying the Sexy,*>* Jessica said as they walked between the ships on the pad, looking for a pinnace similar to the *Sexy*. *<We're flying the…*Maiden Starlight.*>*

<The what?> Sabrina asked. *<Oh, I see. I shouldn't have asked.>*

Jessica couldn't help but laugh. *<Yeah, you really shouldn't have.>*

<I've stripped the Maiden Starlight's *Ident,>* Iris advised. *<Good pick, it has a similar profile to the* Sexy. *Wouldn't fool anyone on a world with more than a dozen monkeys running their ATC, but it shouldn't be a problem here.>*

As Jessica and Nance approached the *Sexy,* the pinnace's ramp lowered, and they rushed onto the ship.

"Iris, or Erin, would one of you ladies get us airborne? Nance and I need to gear up."

<Already on it,> Iris said as the pinnace's ramp closed behind them and the ship lifted into the air on its grav drive.

The two women walked into the second cabin, and Nance activated the door into the secret armory. Little more than a closet, it was stocked well enough to outfit four people in light armor, and tactical gear.

"Glad to get out of this," Jessica said as she pulled the dress off.

"Why?" Nance asked with a wink as she undressed.

"As if you have to ask," Jessica retorted. "Having to wear a long, flowing dress is the second-worst thing that's happened today."

<As if you have anyone to blame but yourself,> Iris chided. *<If you weren't intent on soaking up the sun in the first place…>*

Jessica didn't respond as she pulled on a matte black kinetic dampening underlayer. Once wrapped in its comforting embrace, she stepped onto the armoring pad.

The machine wrapped the ablative plating around her body, then added weapon mounts and ammo pouches. Once the process was complete, it placed the helmet-seal collar around her neck. Directly across from her, Nance was undergoing the same process. They watched each other without speaking, making sure the armoring system did everything properly.

Once it was complete, they stepped off the pads in unison and selected their weapons from the rack.

"Let's try to keep it to quiet stuff," Jessica advised as she grabbed a flechette pistol, a pulse pistol, and a pair of vibr-blades, a new toy she'd picked up a few systems back. She slid the vibr-blades into slots built into her armor's thigh-plates and considered rifle options.

"You should at least have a pulse rifle," Nance advised. "We may have to fight our way through locals to get out of there."

"Yeah, just trying to decide on straight pulse, or a multi-mode."

Nance grabbed one of the multi-mode rifles and handed it to Jessica. "Seriously. You know you want the boom-stick, just take it."

Jessica grabbed the weapon with a laugh and hooked it onto her back.

<We're seven minutes out,> Iris chimed in. *<I got a pad close, but not too close, to the Peerless Transport shuttle. We're cradle 107, they're 143, about a klick away. We're in the long-term layover section, so it should be close to vacant at this time of day.>*

"Works for me," Jessica replied as she picked up a helmet. "Gonna grab a bite before we set down."

"Good call," Nance agreed. "Haven't had anything since my chocolate martini at the bar."

Jessica glanced at Nance. "Really? Dirtside *and* a quintuple threat? I'm impressed."

"Cargo and Trever rated it six-x." Nance grinned.

"It's like you're all grown up, Nance."

Seven minutes later, Jessica stood at the top of the ramp, pulling her helmet on as Nance rushed up, still chewing.

"Butter was frozen," she said with a grin.

Jessica shook her head, and waited for Nance to seat her helmet before they walked down the ramp into the deepening dusk.

They stood between two long rows of smaller shuttles and pinnaces. Most were dark and appeared unoccupied, though a few—such as the *Sexy*—illuminated the area around them with their running lights.

<This is our first time out, isn't it?> Jessica asked Nance as they casually strolled along the illuminated path running between the ships.

<Our first? Jess, we get into dustups several times a year.>

<I mean our first that's just you and I, Nance. Usually more of the crew is along,> Jessica replied.

<Huh…you may be right. Usually Trevor's with you, bustin' heads.> Nance's mental tone was whimsical. *<I'm usually back on the ship, or running some sort of distraction. Nice to be out here on the front lines for a change.>*

<It was just the two of you in that fight back on Treya,> Erin supplied. *<Rest of the crew was back on the ship.>*

Jessica laughed softly. *<Erin, fights that break out at soccer matches don't count. You might as well count going out for supper together.>*

<Which we've almost never done—just you and I,> Nance said, her voice quiet.

<Shit, Nance, I'm sorry. I was always under the impression that you were happy not being dragged along on every outing.>

Nance shrugged. *<Most of the time that's true. Sometimes….>*

<I'll make sure I ask more.>

Iris flashed a warning over their HUDs. *<I read a pair of footfalls ahead. The probes I've sent out haven't made it far enough to get a visual, but they sound heavy.>*

<Could be guards,> Jessica said.

<That's what I was implying, captain obvious,> Iris retorted.

Nance ducked behind the nearest docking cradle hiding in the shadows of a light shuttle, the name *Fearless Bubbly* painted on its side.

Being armed and armored on the pad wasn't a problem—many of the ships employed private security. However, the spaceport's regulations stated all guards had to be registered and screened by the port authority.

Jessica and Nance had been through neither of those processes.

The footfalls grew closer, turned a corner, and two armored guards came into view. They walked through an opening between the rows of ships, and turned down the row Jessica and Nance were in.

Jessica looked behind the shuttle beneath which they were crouched and studied the concrete wall separating the rows. She and Nance could make it over, but it would put them directly in view of surveillance not yet disabled by the Iris's probes.

<*If they spot us, we'll have to take them down,*> Jessica said.

<*We'll just be real quiet-like,*> Nance replied. <*Our gear should keep us invisible on any scanners they're using. They'll need to employ the ole Mark 1 eyeball to spot us.*>

The guards drew closer, and the two women stood rock-still in the shadow of the shuttle, when a tingle ran across Jessica's skin and she sneezed.

Her helmet muffled the sound, but she shifted and her foot twisted, kicking out a small pebble out from underneath. The rock made a loud *pling* as it hit one of the cradle's struts, and the feed from the probes showed the pair of guards had stopped.

<*Shit, Jessica, I thought you were the pro.*>

<*I don't know what that was…I've been getting some weird tingles in my skin lately. They've never made me sneeze before.*>

<*Jess, your skin is artificial and filled with alien microbes…if you get weird tingles, you need to tell me or Finaeus so we can check you out,*> Nance admonished.

<*Hey Nance, I've been getting—*>

<*Not funny, Jessica!*>

The two guards were approaching the shuttle and Jessica straightened. <*I guess we'll have to take them out.*>

<*Sucks,*> Iris commented. <*I'm not sure if I can fake their check-ins from all the right spots. Someone's going to notice they're missing.*>

The guards were within twenty meters of the shuttle when Nance reached up and pulled off her helmet. <*Take your helmet off, Jess; put it and your gun behind me, the landing strut will obscure them.>*

<*What are you thinking?*> Jessica asked as she quickly complied, leaning past Nance to set her rifle against the strut.

As she did, Nance grabbed the collar of Jessica's armor and pulled her close, planting her lips on Jessica's. Then her hands were in Jessica's hair, pulling it free to cascade around their faces.

<*Roll with it, Jessica,*> Nance said.

<*Nance, this'll never work, they're not going to buy it—damn, you're a good kisser, though. Why have we never done this before?*>

"Because you're celibate," Nance whispered as she pulled her lips away from Jessica's for a moment.

"Not you too," Jessica replied with a soft groan. "Seriously, though, a six-x threat, and now this? What's come over you today?"

One of the guards came into view a second later, hand on her pistol.

"Hey! You two, what are you—"

Nance and Jessica turned their heads, but kept their bodies pressed together, hoping the darkness and their proximity would hide the quality of their armor.

"What does it look like we're doing?" Jessica asked.

"Shit!" The guard swore. "You two scared the piss outta me. What are you two doing under there?"

The other guard came around the far side of the shuttle shaking her head. "Can't get one patrol done without someone fucking under a ship."

"You two registered?" the first guard asked. "You can't be out here armed and armored otherwise."

"We're from the *Scared Aphrodite,*" Jessica said, rattling off one of the larger merchant ships she'd seen on the listings when they'd come in. "Captain Tony doesn't like fraternization, so we ducked out after our shift. Look, we'll get back, but can we just have a few more minutes?"

The two guards shared a look and the first one sighed. "You know we can't do that."

Nance gestured to a small pouch on her hip. "Could I provide some sort of persuasion for some leeway? We'll be gone before your next round. We promise."

The second guard laughed. "How much persuasion?"

Nance slowly popped open the pouch and pulled out a pair of local hundred dollar chits. "How's this look?"

The first guard looked at the second and shrugged. "Looks like these lovergirls just bought us our drinks for the next few nights." She reached out and took the chits from Nance's hand and tossed one to the second guard.

"Sounds good to me," the second guard grinned as she snatched the chit out of the air.

Jessica tensed. This was where the two guards would do one of three things: walk away, demand more money, or take them in regardless of the bribe.

Thankfully the pair of women chose option one and walked away, both throwing knowing looks over their shoulders at Jessica and Nance before turning past the shuttles and disappearing from view.

<*I really didn't expect that to work so well,*> Nance said as she reached down and picked up her helmet.

Jessica grinned as she pulled her hair back up. <*And I didn't expect you to be such a good kisser. Do you always keep a few hundred in hard credit on you?*>

<*Of course.*> Nance winked as she slid her helmet back over her head. <*Not everyone can fight their way out of every situation like you do.*>

A minute later the pair was back on the move, this time working their way behind the row of shuttles, along the concrete wall. When they came to a break in the barrier, they crossed into the next row of shuttles, and made their way down it to another intersection where they turned left.

<*Just down there,*> Iris said, highlighting the Peerless Transport shuttle on their HUDs.

The vessel was a sleek, white oval, fifty meters in length. An airlock stood closed at the top of the cradle's ramp, and several lights on the ship illuminated the area around the vessel.

Jessica and Nance kept to the rear of the row of shuttles on the opposite side of the central path, watching the ship for any signs of activity.

<*EM is low,*> Erin said. <*If anyone* **is** *aboard, they're not doing anything.*>

<*I think that if our quarry was here they'd already be taking off,*> Nance said. <*Getting to their super-secret ship up on the moon.*>

<*Or it's a trap,*> Jessica said.

<*Sorry, thought that option went without saying.*>

Iris dispersed a fresh batch of nano that reached out toward the ship, drifting on the breeze so as not to attract any attention. After a minute they began to settle on the shuttle's hull.

<*No countermeasures,*> Erin commented.

<*Yet,*> Iris added.

Then nano slowly worked their way across the skin of the ship toward the airlock control panel, and when they arrived, a batch filtered in through the seams around the panel and tapped into the controls.

<*OK, let's see what we have here,*> Iris said as she began to probe the shuttle's security. <*A bit better than what we've seen most places down here on Ferra. Looks like Peerless actually gives a crap about their stuff.*>

<*So it'll take you what…thirty seconds to crack?*> Nance asked with a soft laugh.

<*Try ten,*> Iris replied. <*The door is mine. How we doing this?*>

<*I'd prefer to know what's in there before we go on in,*> Jessica replied.

<*Seems wise,*> Nance added.

No sooner had they spoken those words, then the probes picked up a pair of footfalls coming from one direction, and loud laughter from the other.

<*Oh for starssakes.*> Jessica muttered.

The ships in this row were lighter, and only four armatures on each cradle supported them. Which meant they wouldn't be able to hide from anything but the most casual observation.

<*Footfall analysis says it's the same two guards.*>

<*Seriously?*> Nance asked. <*Do they patrol at lightspeed or something?*>

Neither of the approaching groups were in visual range yet, and Jessica tapped Nance on the shoulder. *<We go. Now.>*

The pair of women rushed across the lane between the ships and up the ramp. Iris opened the airlock as they approached and closed it the moment they were inside.

Jessica watched the feeds relayed from the nano outside the shuttle. The same two guards came into view on the left, and a group of men and women passed by the intersection on the right.

Neither slowed, and a minute later the row was clear once more.

<I've some probes inside the ship. Nothing so far. Ready to cycle the lock?>

<Yes, let's do it,> Jessica replied.

The inner door on the airlock cycled open and they stepped into the shuttle.

It was a standard configuration—there were only so many ways to make shuttles, after all. Jessica and Nance stood at the edge of a wide main deck, rows of seats filling the space. A staircase in the center of the deck led up to a second level, and to their left was a food service area, beyond which was the entrance to the cockpit.

<Jess! Nance! She's here!> Iris exclaimed suddenly. *<Second level, in a stasis pod!>*

<That explains how whoever did this was able to keep Cheeky and Piya under wraps for so long,> Nance said as she took a step forward.

Jessica held an arm out, stopping Nance. *<This is obviously a trap. Iris needs to check everything before we take*

another step. We've not seen anyone in Orion space use stasis pods. Whoever we're dealing with is a major player.>

<Maybe it is one of these Widows who work for the Orion Guard,> Erin suggested.

<Or any other blackops team,> Jessica added. *<You know a government the size of Orion's probably has hundreds of secret organizations within it. Stars, even the local governments have them.>*

<Right, but they don't have stasis tech,> Erin countered. *<Or if they do, then we probably need to worry about them more than we currently bother to.>*

While they waited for Iris to scan the main deck for any traps, Jessica surveyed the space, looking for anything out of the ordinary.

All-in-all, it was a very plain shuttle. Capable of carrying roughly one hundred fifty passengers, with two human attendants and four automatons.

<I wonder why they'd bring this thing down, rather than their own ship,> Nance asked. *<I would imagine that it would be a lot harder to break into.>*

<Maybe they don't want us making a mess of their ship,> Erin suggested.

<That only makes sense if it's a trap.> Jessica replied.

Iris gave a low chuckle. *<Oh, it's a trap alright. There's a set of grav emitters right at the foot of the staircase. Would have knocked you two flat. Checking the upper deck now.>*

<Check the back,> Jessica directed Nance. *<I'll take a peek in the cockpit.>*

<I think I would have spotted someone if they were here,> Iris said.

Jessica let Nance continue to walk forward, and only when she was a dozen paces away, did Jessica step out and walk toward the cockpit. If there were more traps, no need for both of them to get caught in the same one.

<Just gives us something to do while you check out the upper deck,> Jessica replied to Iris as she walked into the serving area. She peered behind the counter, and checked some of the larger cabinets. An automaton stood in a corner, a skinned model, made to look human. It wore a Peerless Transport uniform, and Jessica walked up to the robot, scanning it with her augmented vision, checking its EM levels and status.

The automaton didn't move, its systems registering a full-powerdown mode when queried.

Jessica turned from the machine and walked into the cockpit. Two main seats were at the front, and a third sat behind and on the left.

The ship could probably fly itself to the moon and back without trouble, but people always liked to know there were people around in case things went wrong—especially here in the retro-zone.

<All clear back here,> Nance reported. *<Just the restrooms and two automatons.>*

Jessica stepped out of the cockpit and back into the food service area. *<One 'ton and an empty cockpit here.>* Something about the automaton bothered her, but she couldn't put her finger on it. She checked again, and the thing hadn't moved a micrometer since she first looked at it, though.

<I've cleared the top deck. Checking over the stasis pod now, but you should be good to come up.>

Jessica walked into the main cabin to see Nance standing close to the foot of the stairs, looking at the space where the disabled grav field trap was.

She glanced back at Jessica. *<Here goes nothing.>*

Nance walked to the stairs and began climbing them without incident. Jessica waited for Nance to reach the top before she followed after, bracing for some sort of attack as she climbed the steps.

None came, and a few seconds later, both women stood on the shuttle's second level, looking at the stasis pod wedged into the aisle at the back of the level.

Nance took one tentative step, then rushed toward it. *<Dang, she's got one hell of a shiner on her right eye.>*

<Give me another minute and I'll have it opened,> Iris cautioned. *<It's a standard sequence, not much different than the models we use on the* Intrepid. *Just looking through initialization procedures to see if there are any surprises.>*

"May I offer you a beverage?" a voice said and Jessica turned to see the upper level's automaton hold up a bottle of water. "Water? Coffee? Wine."

"No," Jessica said. "Resume standby."

The automaton nodded and reached under the counter. "Restadia wine. One glass or two."

Jessica shook her head and took a step toward the automaton. "Dammit, stupi—"

<DUCK!> Erin yelled, and Jessica dropped without any hesitation as a pulse shot rippled through the air where her head had been and struck the overhead, shattering a light fixture.

<It's coming up the stairs,> Erin reported.

Jessica jumped behind the bar, pushing the automaton over, while Nance ducked behind a row of seats.

<***What's*** *coming up the stairs?*> Jessica asked as a shadow appeared to float over the railing. It dropped behind the seats and disappeared from view.

<*What the hell is that?*> Nance asked.

Jessica unslung her pulse rifle and fired a series of blasts at the seats. The concussive waves would be slowed, but would still hit whoever was on the far side.>

<*Looks like we have one of Misha's widows on our hands.*>

POOL WITH A VIEW

STELLAR DATE: 03.10.8948 (Adjusted Years)
LOCATION: Killashandra Mountain Resort, Ferra, Sullus System
REGION: Midway Cluster, Orion Freedom Alliance Space

"So much for the bad guys always being in the bar," Trevor said as he and Cargo walked through the room, scanning the patrons' faces to see if any matched the *Laren*'s crew roster.

"I didn't say they were *always* in the bar. I just said that since it was nearby, we may as well check there." Cargo stopped at the end of the room and sighed. "Well, I guess we'll move on to plan B."

Trevor opened his mouth to reply, when the sound of the opening break on a pool table came through a doorway to their left.

"Looks like there's still more bar to check out," Cargo said with a wink.

The two men walked through the door to see a pool hall with at least forty tables spread throughout the space. A few games were going on, but none of the *Laren*'s crew were in evidence.

Cargo sapped his fingers. "Damn, got my hopes up."

They turned to leave but the sound of another break reached their ears. Cargo looked around the room, not seeing any games that had just started.

"Back there," Trevor pointed across the hall. "Looks like private rooms, or something."

"Here's hoping redux," Cargo said as they threaded the tables and approached the doors at the rear of the pool hall. There were three in total. Two were closed, but one was open a crack.

Trevor nodded to Cargo. *<Just walk in? Who first?>*

<I'll go first,> Cargo replied. *<I'll do the ol' 'is this a private party?' routine.>*

Cargo stepped ahead of Trevor, and when he reached the door, pushed it wide and walked into the room before stopping and looking around.

The room was occupied by Captain Hunter and three officers from the *Laren.*

"Oh, shoot, wrong room," Cargo said, raising a hand and taking a step back.

<Cargo, they don't look surprised at all,> Hank cautioned.

<Yeah, I see that.>

"As unlikely as it seems," Captain Hunter said from the far end of the table said as she raised a handgun. "You're in exactly the right place."

Cargo's smile disappeared as he took a step forward. "Captain Hunter, you have ten seconds to hand over Cheeky."

"The what?" Hunter cocked her head. "Are you calling me cheeky? That doesn't even make any sense.

Cargo took another step forward, but spotted motion out of he corner of his eye. He spun to see a massive woman emerge from behind the door, bearing down on him, barrel-sized fists swinging toward his head

He dodged the first swing, but then one of the *Laren*'s officers grabbed him from behind. Cargo wrenched to the side, trying to pull away.

The massive woman pulled her fist back to swing at Cargo again, when a pink and blue blur streaked through the doorway and crashed. into the massive woman. The impact slammed her into the pool table, pushing it backward and pinning Captain Hunter between it and the far wall.

"Fuck, Jenny!" Captain Hunter called out.

Cargo took advantage of the distraction to wrench himself free from the man holding him, and swung a fist at the officer's face.

A shot rang out, and Cargo felt something whiz by his ear. He turned, saw Hunter taking aim at him again, and ducked behind the officer he was fighting.

Hunter held off shooting, and Cargo punched the man he was using for cover in the kidneys before lifting him bodily and rushing toward the *Laren*'s captain.

As Cargo ran, he glanced across the pool table and saw Trevor picking up a pair of pool balls which he then smashed into the massive woman's face.

She reeled backward while Trevor turned to face the other two officers—one of whom was firing point-blank shots from a pulse pistol at Trevor's torso.

A rage-filled bellow tore its way out of Trevor's throat, and he grabbed the shooter's wrist and yanked hard, sending the man flying across the room.

Cargo's attention was drawn back to the man he was using as a shield, who had twisted and was now punching him in the side. Cargo gave a heave and threw the man toward the captain. He missed, and the man hit the wall next to Captain Hunter.

With his own rage-filled bellow, Cargo lunged at Hunter, trying to wrest her pistol away.

She was ready for him and fired a shot before he made it half-way. The projectile struck Cargo in the left shoulder, but he didn't slow. A pool ball rolled across the table and Cargo grabbed it, taking a cue from Trevor.

Cargo drew his arm back to throw the ball, but Hunter didn't waver, the barrel of her gun trained on his head.

"Don't move, scumbag," she yelled, and Cargo lowered his raised arm. "That's right, buddy you're—"

Hunter's utterance was cut short by another pool ball striking her in the sternum with a resounding crack.

She spasmed and the gun fired, hitting the table right beside Cargo. He reached out and grabbed the pistol, wrenching it from her hands before training it on her.

"Thanks, Trevor," Cargo said as he backed away from Captain Hunter.

Trevor threw another pool ball, past Cargo, hitting the first officer in the head as he rose from where Cargo had thrown him.

A long shaky breath escaped Cargo's lips and he glanced at the door, which had been shut at some point during the scuffle.

<Is anyone coming to investigate, Hank?>

<No…strangely. I think our fair Captain Hunter here may have paid someone off to ignore any ruckus.>

Cargo turned back to the *Laren*'s captain, who was taking short, shallow breaths with one hand on her sternum.

"So, Captain Hunter, like I said before: where's Cheeky?"

"What…" Hunter wheezed, "the fuck…are you talking about?"

"You know our pilot, the crew member you abducted in Parda City?"

Hunter frowned. "I have no clue who that is. I've never been to Parda City. We were approached by a woman this afternoon to keep an eye out for you. If we saw you, there was a considerable bounty to be collected."

Cargo gestured with the gun he was holding. "And you always play pool while armed?"

"Well, she did say this was your favorite table."

"Shit, Cargo, have we been played?" Trevor asked.

<I can drop some nano on these four and put them to sleep,> Hank offered. *<They're too retro-zone to have any defenses.>*

<OK, you do that, Hank. Trevor, get outside and see if you can link up to the satcomm network. If this was a decoy, then Sabrina *is in trouble.>*

Trevor nodded and rushed out of the room toward the bar's outside deck.

"So there's no bounty on you?" Captain Hunter asked in a hoarse whisper.

"Well, not that I know of," Cargo replied as he kept the gun fixed on her.

<One down,> Hank announced.

Hunter frowned. "Then what the hell is going on?"

"Well, if you didn't abduct Cheeky, then we both just got played. What are you doing in the Sullus System, anyway? It's not on your usual route."

The woman coughed and then groaned, pushing her head back against the wall. "We got a last-minute shipment for this system. Was a good commission. Then we spotted a deal for a week here at Killashandra, and decided it was time to get a bit of R&R."

Cargo shook his head and walked around the table to take a look at the other two officers. "Sounds like you were set up to set us up."

Hunter nodded, apparently out of words for the time being.

Satisfied that Hunter's three officers, and the massive woman—Jenny if he recalled Hunter's yell earlier—were all out cold, he walked to the captain's side and pulled the pool table back a few centimeters.

"C'mon out," he said, waving her forward with the gun.

"What're you going to do now?" Captain Hunter asked.

"Wait for Trevor. Then maybe take a look at your shuttle."

Hunter scowled. "Why? You plan to steal it?"

"No, we're looking for Cheeky, remember? I'm not just going to take you at your word that you don't know who she is."

"Who names their kid Cheeky?" Hunter asked as she leaned against the pool table.

Cargo shrugged. "No one, I imagine. She named herself that."

"Really? Who na—"

"Shut up, Hunter."

<*Want me to knock her out too?*> Hank asked.

<*No. We'll see what Trevor comes back with. We may also need her to get us the codes for her shuttle.*>

They waited in silence—except for Hunter's wheezing—until Trevor burst back into the room a minute later.

"I couldn't raise them!" he said in a rush.

"The satcomm link no good?" Cargo asked.

Trevor shook his head, worry evident in his eyes. "Link was good, just can't raise anyone. Sabrina, Jessica, no one's answering."

"Shit!" Cargo swore. "Captain Hunter, looks like we'll be making use of your shuttle after all."

TAKE DOWN

STELLAR DATE: 03.10.8948 (Adjusted Years)
LOCATION: Parda City Spaceport, Ferra, Sullus System
REGION: Midway Cluster, Orion Freedom Alliance Space

Finaeus placed the coffee pot back on its stand and picked up his cup. Delicious black goodness, just waiting for him to consume.

In the case for proving the existence of god, so far as he was concerned, coffee was exhibit A. Maybe. Sex might be exhibit A, but coffee was a close second.

Thinking of sex brought Finaeus's mind right to thoughts of Cheeky, and that was a place he couldn't go. Not if he wanted to stay focused.

At any moment, Nance and Jessica might need them. Either to gather intel, or ride to the rescue. No option, or effort was off the table. Push come to shove, he'd demand Sabrina unleash her full arsenal to save Cheeky.

Not that he thought he'd have to push hard. He could tell the ship's AI was beside herself with worry.

Finaeus poured a second cup for Misha and grabbed a couple of pastries from the basket on the table before walking back out into the corridor. He turned toward the ladder, but then stopped short; there was no way he could manage two cups plus the food.

Why on Earth did that niece of mine never get stairs put in here? He thought before turning back toward the lift at the far end of the passageway.

Something caught his eye as he walked back past the galley. A shadow on the wall that shouldn't be there.

"Fuck!" Finaeus hollered, and threw his coffee at the shadow before turning and running back to the ladder. He reached it a second later and scrambled up to the command deck.

Finaeus slipped on the last rung, and his shin struck the deck. He struggled to his feet just as something grabbed his ankle and pulled him down.

"Oh, hell no!" Finaeus shouted and kicked out with his other foot, connecting with something that gave out a wheezing sound.

<Finaeus!> Sabrina exclaimed. *<Something opened the—oh crap, it's inside!>*

"I know, Sabrina," Finaeus grunted as he raced toward the bridge's entrance, and threw himself across the threshold. He signaled the door to close, but it was too late as an invisible weight landed atop him.

"Freeze!" Sabrina's voice thundered through the bridge and an autoturret lowered, firing a kinetic round at the shifting blur over Finaeus.

The amorphous shape flickered and resolved into the form of a woman, covered head to toe in a gleaming black sheath—except her head which was a featureless oval. For a moment, no one moved, then Finaeus felt a knife at his side.

"Think you can shoot me before I gut him?" the attacker asked in an ethereal-sounding hiss.

"Yes!" Sabrina shouted at the same time that Finaeus cried out. "Stop!"

<Why stop?>

<Because we want intel, not corpses,> Finaeus replied as he looked around for Misha. *<Where are you, Misha?>*

<In the can! What should I do?>

<Stay put,> Sabrina said. *<I have a plan.>*

"It's been a long time," the woman said.

"It has?" Finaeus asked. "Do I know you? Did I cut you in line at the deli or something?"

"Yes, you certainly do know me, Finaeus Tomlinson. Can you imagine how surprising it was to see you this deep in Orion?"

"Not as surprising as it is to *not* see you," Finaeus grunted, keenly aware of the knife-blade biting into his skin.

"You don't recognize the sound of my voice?" the woman asked.

Finaeus had to admit, there was something familiar, but it was also strange, like the speaker was breathing in while uttering each word.

The woman leant in close and whispered in Finaeus's ear. "And here you said that you'd never forget those nights we spent together on Europa. I thought they meant something to you."

Finaeus felt the blood drain from his face and his breath caught in is throat. "L—Lisa?"

The woman laughed—though it sounded closer to gasping.

"Show me your face," Finaeus said—half buying time for whatever Sabrina was planning, and half desperate to see the woman again. "I can't believe you're still alive…it's been two thousand years since we last—"

"Since you walked out on me?" Lisa asked. "C'mon, say it. You walked out on *me*."

"Lisa…you were siding with Kirkland. I had to stand beside my brother." Finaeus didn't speak the other reason; that Lisa was often verbally abusive with their daughter, Sandra.

"And look where that got you. I heard you were exiled—or ran off. The stories vary. Just didn't think you ran off to Orion. You should have looked me up."

Lisa snorted the last and Finaeus reached up to touch the smooth faceplate of his ex-wife's helmet.

"Take this off. Let me look at you."

"No!" Lisa jerked her head back.

Finaeus wondered what Lisa was hiding. He also wondered why she hadn't attacked him with nano yet—though he hadn't tried to infiltrate her either.

"You didn't expect to find me here," he said after a moment. "This wasn't about me at all…."

Lisa shook her head. "Not initially, no, though you're an excellent prize. But this ship and its shield technology is the real goal."

"What do you know about that," Sabrina asked sharply.

"We had agents at Bollam's World," Lisa replied. "We saw what you did to that pirate fleet and their shield umbrella. And though it took awhile to get the truth about Marsalla out of RHY, when we got the logs, it became all too clear what ship had been responsible for destroying that world…*Sabrina*."

"So RHY *was* developing bioweapons for the Orion Guard," Finaeus said. "I can't believe Kirkland went along with that. He's always been a proponent of a more conventional conflict."

Lisa leant in close to Finaeus, pressing her body into his. Old memories flooded back, recollections their past exploits. He remembered her over him like this, her long white hair pooling on either side of his face. Good times from before the FTL wars, before the retreat and the schism.

"What Praetor Kirkland doesn't know won't hurt him," Lisa whispered. "Much."

"There's a reason why we don't make weapons like that, Lisa," Finaeus retorted. "They're species killers. Namely humanity."

"Don't be naïve, Finaeus," Lisa tittered. "You're the ones protecting New Canaan, with their picotech. They're the real risk, them and your precious Airtha—though I suppose she may not be so precious to you, if the reasons for your exile are to be believed."

<Were you married to this woman, Finaeus?> Sabrina asked. *<She talks to you like you were married.>*

<Yeah, twice. It's a long story.>

Sabrina chuckled. *<I bet it was. She seems a bit…off.>*

<I've noticed that too. So, do you have some sort of special plan?>

<Oh, of course!> Sabrina replied. *<I just didn't want to interrupt your special moment.>*

<Please, interrupt away.>

"Hey Finaeus," Cheeky said, appearing over Lisa's shoulder. "You going to have sex with this woman, or should I pull her off you?"

Lisa turned her head, a look of shock on it. "What? You're—"

A pulse blast shot out from one of the autoturrets, knocking Lisa off Finaeus.

With tremendous grace—for someone whose bones should feel like they're the clapper in a bell—Lisa rolled with the pulse blast and came up behind Cheeky, the knife previously at Finaeus's side held to Cheeky's throat.

"Enough, Finaeus. Give me the command codes for this ship or I kill this woman."

"So that's good news," Sabrina said. "You haven't already killed her yet. Means I won't kill you—yet."

"What?" Lisa asked as Cheeky reached over her shoulder and grabbed Lisa's neck with both hands, bending over and lifting the assassin into the air.

Finaeus watched in terror as Lisa jerked the knife blade across Cheeky's throat before sailing across the bridge where multiple blasts from the bridge's turrets hit her.

Finaeus rose on shaky legs and frowned; no blood seeped from the gash on Cheeky's neck. Realization hit him, and he gave a grim smile. "Thanks Addie. Are you OK?"

The AHAP nodded. "I believe so, nothing vital appears to be damaged."

"Good," Finaeus replied as he walked around the scan console to see Lisa crumpled on the ground, moaning softly.

<*Stay back from her,*> Sabrina cautioned.

<*Yeah, I know…she's more than a little dangerous.*>

"Get that creepy-ass helmet off. Now!" Finaeus ordered his ex-wife.

"Fuck you, Finaeus," Lisa whispered. Then her voice grew stronger. "This is all your fault. If you hadn't sided with your power-hungry brother, we would still be together."

"Living in Kirkland's utopia, eh?" Finaeus asked. "How's that working out?"

"Better than living with the abomination that is Airtha," Lisa shot back.

"Last warning, Lisa. Take off the helmet, or Sabrina fills you with holes."

<You can't really fill someone with holes, its oxymoronic,> Sabrina said privately.

<Sabs—>

<Sorry.>

Another series of pulse blasts shot out of the turrets, hitting Lisa in the stomach.

"Have some internal bleeding, you stupid woman," Sabrina said aloud. "I bet I can crush your lower body and Finaeus still can take what he needs from your mind. Or you can just comply."

Lisa raised a hand in surrender, and touched her neck on one side, and then the other. A second later, her helmet split in two and fell to the floor.

Finaeus gasped and took a step back.

"Was she this hideous when you were married to her, Finaeus?" Sabrina asked after a moment's awkward silence. "I always thought you were more shallow than that."

He didn't respond, taking in the ruin of the woman he had once given his life to. Her skin was alabaster white, appearing transparent in places. She was entirely hairless, not even eyelashes graced her wrinkled eyelids. Her ears were gone, and two long slits sat in the middle of her face—where her nose should be.

White, thin lips twisted into a toothless smile. "Time hasn't been as kind to me as it has to you."

Lisa's voice sounded even more ethereal without the helmet. As though it had come from a long way away and was only echoing out of her.

"What happened to you?" Finaeus asked when the power of speech finally returned to him. "How…why…."

Lisa pressed her lips together and shook her head.

Silence fell between on the bridge once more, until Misha's voice came over the link.

<Can I come out of the head yet?>

* * * * *

Jessica fired another pulse blast at the seats where the shadow had disappeared before edging out past the bar.

Nothing moved and only the sound of the bar automaton trying to right itself could be heard.

She peered down the first two rows of seats, which were empty, and then crept to the one at the front at the level, which was clear as well.

<Where the hell?> Jessica asked, turning with her back against the ship's bulkhead, before moving past the final row.

A pulse shot rang out, and Jessica turned to see Nance flung backward to hit the ship's rear wall before falling to the ground.

Jessica caught sight of the shadow for a moment, a shifting mass near the top of the stairs, then it was gone again.

There were only so many routes for the enemy to take, and Jessica took two steps toward the bar, turned, and held out her hand, emitting a piezoelectric pulse at the same moment a pulse blast rolled through the air toward her.

The wave of energy from her hand overpowered the pulse wave, and slammed into the shadow, coalescing it into the shape of a woman.

Jessica didn't wait to see what else this mysterious figure had in her arsenal. She rushed toward the Widow, while drawing energy from the microbes in her skin. When they collided, she sent a burst of energy into Cheeky and Piya's abductor.

The woman in black screamed in a strange breathy voice, but took a swing at Jessica and tried to shove her back. Jessica didn't hesitate to hit her again, and again, and on the fourth blast of energy the woman in black fell to the ground.

<Shit, Jess, I think you cooked her,> Nance said as she rose on unsteady legs. *<I hope she's not dead.>*

Jessica looked down at the slow rise and fall of the woman's chest.

<No, she's not. Not yet at least.>

<In related news,> Iris interjected. *<I've activated stasis shutdown. Cheeky will be with you in thirty seconds.>*

Jessica knelt beside the woman and looked for a latch or something on her helmet. It seemed to mesh seamlessly with her armor. She dropped a batch of nano on it, some of the last infiltration bots she possessed, and they wormed their way between the helmet and the suit. A seam highlighted on Jessica's vision as the nano worked their way around highlighting small buttons on each side.

A gentle push on each, and the helmet cracked open, splitting down the middle.

<That was easy,> Erin commented. *<You must have fried it.>*

Jessica nodded silently as she prised the helmet apart and then sat back, staring at the strange apparition within.

"What the hell?" she exclaimed.

"What the hell is right?" Cheeky's voice came from the rear of the shuttle. "Where the heck are we? I didn't go on a crazy bender did I?"

REGROUP

STELLAR DATE: 03.11.8948 (Adjusted Years)
LOCATION: Parda City Spaceport, Ferra, Sullus System
REGION: Midway Cluster, Orion Freedom Alliance Space

Finaeus and Misha waited at the main bay doors as the *Sexy* set down next to *Sabrina.* The pinnace's ramp slowly lowered, and Finaeus jogged down the gantry to the ground.

Jessica appeared first and the figure she carried stopped Finaeus dead in his tracks.

It was Lisa. Another horribly disfigured Lisa.

"What the actual fuck," he whispered.

"You like our little prize?" Jessica asked with a sour grin. "We got her at the bottom of the cracker box we found Cheeky in."

"Looks like we're collecting the whole set," Finaeus replied.

Jessica's brow furrowed. "What do you mean?"

Then Cheeky came down the ramp, and Finaeus rushed past Jessica and crashed into the young woman, wrapping her in his arms and lifting her into the air.

"Easy, easy," Cheeky said as she leant her head forward and rested it on his shoulder. "I'm fine. Just a sucker punch in the eye and some sort of suppression net."

"Dammit, Cheeky," Finaeus said. "You had me worried half to death."

<Us too,> Piya said. *<But here we are, cute and sexy as always…OK, I'm cute, she's sexy.>*

Nance followed Cheeky off the shuttle and patted her on the shoulder. "Let's get you into the ship, I want to run a quick checkup. Make sure there aren't any surprises inside you."

"You never let go of the whole, 'you could be terribly infected' thing, do you, Nance?"

"Nope, and we're all still alive because of it. Now, let's get in."

They stepped away from the pinnace as its ramp closed up and the ship lifted into the air once more.

"Did we get a new crewmember? Who's flying the pinnace?" Finaeus asked.

<*I am,*> Iris answered. <*For all Jessica's 'I'm a real pilot in the deep black' talk, I fly the damn thing more than she does.*>

He walked up the ramp into *Sabrina*, where Jessica—still holding her Lisa—stopped and turned.

"OK, Fin, what do you mean about the whole set?"

"Didn't Sabrina tell you on the way back?" Finaeus asked.

<*I was trying to keep it on the down-low. We don't know who could be listening on Ferra's nets,*> Sabrina joined in the conversation. <*One of these clone assassins managed to slip right in through the lower maintenance hatch. Misha and I are scanning all our systems to make sure she didn't leave any presents.*>

"Clones?" Jessica asked.

Finaeus let out a sigh of relief as he looked at this second Lisa's face. "Must be. Stars in heaven, what have you been up to, Lisa?"

"Lisa?" Nance asked as she led Cheeky past them toward the medbay. "You know her? Them?"

"This is a lot of random questions," Jessica said. "Can someone explain what's going on?"

<*Lisa is Finaeus's ex-wife. Now we have two Lisas. Though I guess if they're clones they're not really Finaeus's ex-wives.*>

Finaeus stared at the Lisa Jessica held, still trying to process what was happening. "She sure acted like it."

Cheeky giggled and looked back at Finaeus. "Talk about having a psycho ex!"

"No ki—" Finaeus began when a shuttle set down in the spot just vacated by the *Sexy*.

"Now what?" he muttered, then spotted the name *Laren III* on the shuttle's tail fin.

<*Hold up, Finaeus,*> Cargo called over the Link.

<*Cargo. Damn, I was worried that the Lisas had backup.*>

<*The who?*>

<*Just get aboard,*> Jessica replied. <*It'll be easier to do this just once as a group.*>

As she spoke, the *Laren III*'s airlock opened up and Trevor walked out, a woman slung over his shoulder. Cargo came through a moment after, and then the shuttle lifted off again before settling down the next row over.

The two men walked up the ramp, Cargo looking sour, and Trevor grinning like a cheshire cat.

"Miss us?" Trevor asked as he walked past Finaeus.

"Yeah, sure. We were all tears and tissues without you." Finaeus rolled his eyes. "Who's the sack of potatoes?"

Cargo spat on the ramp before stepping onto the ship. "Captain of the *Laren*. We brought her as insurance, but seems like Jessica and Nance already managed to find Cheeky *and* her abductor."

"And Sabs and I defended the ship against infiltration," Finaeus added with a grin. "What'd you two do?"

"Beat the stuffing out of some pissant freighter dickheads who thought they were hot shit," Trevor said and then patted the ass of the woman held over his shoulder. "Gonna mount this one's head on my wall."

"Trevor!" Jessica cried out with a gagging sound. "That's…just disturbing."

Trevor chuckled. "Yeah, I guess that's kinda gross when you say it aloud. It was funnier in my head."

"Seriously," Finaeus said. "Why'd you bring her?"

"Well, until two minutes ago, we thought she was going to lead us to whoever hired her, and then to Cheeky."

<*Yeah, we have Cheeky back now,*> Sabrina supplied. <*I was going to send you a message. But then I saw the second Lisa. I was just explaining that there could be more, so didn't want to send a message over the planet's networks.*>

Cargo held a hand up in frustration. "What in the stars are these Lisas everyone keeps talking about?"

<*Come up to the bridge,*> Sabrina said. <*We should leave Ferra. There could be more of those Lisas out there.*>

"I booked our departure on the way over," Jessica said as she walked across the bay and wrapped her arms around Trevor. "You look like shit, hon. Your trophy has a nice ass, though. Is that the part you want to mount?"

"Whoa, too much double entendre for me there," Trevor said with a laugh.

"Put her in Hold 3," Cargo said. "Everyone, meet on the bridge in ten. I need to clean up first."

*****

Jessica was the last one to walk onto the bridge, freshly showered and back in her favorite purple shipsuit.

"Took your time," Cargo grunted.

"You said we had ten minutes," Jessica said as she sat at her console.

"It's been almost fifteen," Cargo replied.

Jessica sighed. "Cargo. Nance and I had to get to the armory to pull our armor off, and then shower. It's a miracle I made it this fast."

"I made it in ten," Nance replied. "I don't need to shower, though—wait, neither do you, Jessica, what are you talking about?"

"When I do a big discharge in armor like that, my skin gets a weird smell. It's hard to describe, like ozone sweat. It's really unpleasant."

"OK, well, now that Jessica's fresh as a daisy—" Cargo began, only to be interrupted by Trevor who leant over and buried his nose in Jessica's hair, taking a long breath. "Trevor…seriously."

"Sorry, it does smell really good."

Cargo sighed. "Sometimes I think I'm the father and you're my unruly brood."

Cheeky was leaning against the back of her pilot's seat and flashed a mischievous smile. "So, if you're the dad, who's the mom? I kinda feel like it would be Jessica. But then she's cheating on you with Trevor."

"I'm *definitely* not the ship's mom," Jessica said with a snort. "Ship's mom is definitely Nance."

"Me!" Nance squeaked. "Why is everyone always calling me mom?"

"Because you do the most scolding," Finaeus said with a wink as he leant over and pinched her arm.

"Fin! Stop that! I'll make you scrub—" Nance stopped as half the crew burst out laughing. She sighed. "OK, maybe you have a point. But dad and I have a purely platonic relationship. Don't go getting any ideas, Cheeky."

Cheeky raised her hands and grinned. "I don't play match maker anymore. I'm monogamous now."

"I don't really see how those two things are related," Jessica said.

<They would all be doomed without us,> Iris said, her tone both wry and mournful.

<You got that right,> Sabrina added. *<I kinda feel like I'm ship's mom, anyway. You have no idea how much I clean up after all of you. It's like you're my own personal parasites.>*

"I'd like to think that we have a more symbiotic relationship," Cheeky said with a wink.

"Great, now that we've got this out of our systems, can we all get up to speed on what the hell is going on?" Cargo asked.

Over the next ten minutes, each group related their experiences and what they'd learned from the Lisas and Captain Hunter.

"You know what this means, right?" Jessica asked, looking around at the crew.

"Yeah," Misha nodded. "We're made. Not only does the Orion Freedom Alliance know we're here, they know *what* ship this is, and they know that good ol' Finaeus is aboard."

"We're close to the inner edge of Orion space," Cheeky said. "We could skip around inhabited systems, not make any more stops 'til we get to the Inner Stars."

<We're at least a year from the Inner Stars, though,> Sabrina said. *<We can't carry that much fuel. We'd have to stop and scoop somewhere.>*

Cheeky brought up a display of the path they'd planned to take to the Inner Stars. "There are a few red dwarfs that don't appear to have any settlements. We could stop at those, scoop fuel off the star or gas giants."

<I think they'd expect that, Cheeky,> Erin replied and a few other routes lit up on the star chart. *<Unless we backtrack, there are only four or five routes to the Inner Stars that we can take using unsettled red dwarf star systems. Orion will expect that.>*

Jessica nodded. "I know I would."

<Plus, the dark layer maps may not be up to date if no one lives at those systems,> Sabrina added.

Cheeky threw her hands into the air. "Well, what are we going to do, then? Just drift home at sublight? See you in ten-thousand years, guys."

"We work out the best route, and take calculated risks," Cargo said. "It's no different than what we've been doing all along."

"We're going to need to get a lot more supplies if we're in the black for a year," Misha said. "Can we postpone our dust-off?"

Cargo shook his head. "No. Like Sabrina said, there could be more of those Lisas around. We need to get gone."

"We need to find out if there *are* more, and what their plan is…was," Jessica added.

"I could talk to her…hers…one of her," Finaeus offered.

<She seemed really upset at you, Finaeus,> Sabrina said. *<Do you really think she'd share what she knows if you talk to her?>*

Finaeus blew out a long breath. "I'm really not sure. Now that I think of it…she'd probably get more out of me than the other way around."

"Mature of you to realize that," Jessica said.

"Look at me, all growed up."

Nance laughed. "And it only took six thousand years."

"How's it feel to know that the enemy has a whole secret task force made up of your ex-wife?" Misha grinned and gave Finaeus a light punch on the shoulder.

"Shit, Misha, like shit. Those aren't my ex-wife, those are clones. And they know they're clones. Which means that they're fucking nuts."

"Why's that?" Misha asked.

"Because," Jessica said as she ran a hand through her hair. "Clones are made for one reason: they're expendable. You can't take a useful human subject, clone them to duplicate that usefulness and let them know they're clones. At best, they're reckless. At worst they kill themselves. En masse. It's happened before."

"What if the source subject was just so good at her job that they could only achieve her skill level with clones?" Cheeky asked. "Then they're not made that way because they're expendable, it's because they're prized."

<It doesn't work that way,> Iris replied. *<People don't treat them the same way because you can always just make another one. Even if they're not intended to be expendable. They are. And even if they're not, the clones think they are, because there's nothing special about them.>*

"Is that why they made her so gross?" Cheeky asked. "All disfigured?"

"It's a form of psychological manipulation. The Lisas's—the Widows," Finaeus said and stopped for a moment. "I'd rather think of her that way. It's more fitting."

Everyone nodded and waited for him to continue.

"The Widows aren't people. They're things. They were created for a specific task. They were made to do a thing and to it well. But their creators wouldn't allow them to have personal attachments. No family, no friends. Nothing. They're hunters and killers."

<But she seemed to have a very personal reaction to you, Finaeus,> Sabrina interjected. *<It wasn't machine-like. It was raw emotion.>*

Finaeus nodded slowly, his lips pressed into a thin line.

"Seeing you must have triggered something," Jessica said. "That would explain why she was so reckless."

"Yeah," Finaeus said in agreement. "That's why you don't use clones. You can condition them all you want, but it's fragile. The wrong stimuli, the wrong thought process and boom. It all falls apart.

"Plus it's slavery," Cheeky added.

Finaeus grunted and shook his head. "That too."

Cargo slowly stroked his chin. "I wonder if there's a chance that these Li—these Widows went rogue. Maybe they didn't report us to their superiors."

"It's possible." Finaeus shrugged.

"Well, then," Jessica said, looking to Cheeky. "Looks like our first stop is the Widow's ship on Ur. We'll see if we can pull anything from their logs. We'll also need to see if we can get anything out of them."

"That's all you," Cargo said to Jessica. "You're our resident cop. You know all about the bright lights and the sharp sharp knives."

"I don't see how you'll get anything out of them," Nance said. "Torture doesn't work—not with people like these."

Jessica snorted. "Not if you do it wrong. It's not about what people say, it's about what they don't say. You talk and talk and watch the things they dance around, or the things they give up too easily."

"Surely a good operative knows that too," Nance said. "It's all misdirection."

"Hints and clues," Jessica replied. "We're not looking for a roadmap. We need hints and clues. We can then correlate that against other stuff, like what we learn from their ship."

<Lift-off is in t-minus fifteen minutes,> Sabrina said. *<I'll book a berth on Ur. Try to get close to the Widows' ship.>*

"What about Captain Hunter?" Trevor asked.

"We'll keep her in the hold for now and dump her when we leave Ur," Cargo replied. "I've left a message for her officers—when they wake up—that their good behavior will ensure her health and wellness."

Jessica pushed off from the console. "I guess I'd best get to work on our guests."

WIDOWSPEAK

STELLAR DATE: 03.11.8948 (Adjusted Years)
LOCATION: Parda City Spaceport, Ferra, Sullus System
REGION: Midway Cluster, Orion Freedom Alliance Space

Sabrina was lifting off from the Parda City Spaceport as Jessica sat down across from the two Widows. The three of them were in a hidden compartment off Hold 7 that possessed strong nano and physical defenses.

Grav fields held the two women suspended in the air, their bodies locked in place by the graviton's tight grip. The grav field was just the first line of defense. Should it fail, stasis would snap into place around the prisoners.

If that didn't hold them, the ten autoturrets in the room would do the trick.

Or Jessica could just fry them herself.

The two Widows didn't speak, their eyes calm and emotionless, long nostril slits flaring slightly as they drew in deep breaths.

"Look at the two of you," Jessica said after they stared at one another for a minute. "You're like a monument to Orion's failings. Their best operatives, unable to take out the crew of one little freighter."

Neither of the Widows spoke, but Two—the one Jessica had fought on the Peerless Transport shuttle—glanced at One for a moment. Perhaps One had jumped the gun boarding Sabrina.

"We matched up your ship with one we spotted four systems back. Is that how long you've been following us? That was just about three months ago."

Again, neither of the Widows replied.

"Finaeus thinks that you found us around then, not earlier. He think's you're too impetuous to hold off for that long. Me? I think you're more patient than he gives you credit for. I mean, you have this whole gleaming black female killing machine thing going on, that implies a lot of skulk-in-the-shadows-and-wait attitude."

Of course, the two Widows were not in their black stealth-suits anymore. Those were safe and secure in a stasis pod—just in case they contained any surprises. The Widows' only clothing now was a simple grey shift for each.

"I guess we shouldn't be surprised," Jessica said with a slow nod. "I mean, you're not idiots, right? Eventually someone had to investigate RHY's screwup at the Naga System. And then *eventually* someone would have realized the ship that hit Marsalla and destroyed the planet was the same ship that had been in Bollam's World—though *Sabrina* looks quite a bit different now, so maybe that wasn't such a certainty."

Neither of the Widows so much as blinked, and Jessica rose from her chair to pace in front of them. "To think of the logistics that would have to be in place to take us down. You'd need a system where you knew we'd be, a way to manage a clean snatch of our ship and Finaeus. Probably me too."

Jessica stopped her pacing and turned to look at the two women. "Oh! That's it! You were *never* after Cheeky. You wanted to hit me, but I went outside at the last minute to do my impression of a sunflower.

"Plan seems weak, though. You had to know that the two of you weren't enough to take this ship and crew. At least not with any real certainty. Which means…"

Jessica stopped to tap her chin before glancing at the two Widows once more. "You ladies are great sounding boards. I should come bounce ideas off you more often. I can't help but think that maybe you jumped the gun. That you were supposed to wait for reinforcements. Either that or you overestimate yourselves. Finaeus said you do that a lot. He said you're prone to rash decisions and poor choices. It was one of the reasons he left you."

"He didn't—" one of the Widows—the one who had boarded *Sabrina*—began, but the other barked, "A93. Stop!"

"A93?" Jessica asked. "What a lovely alphanumeric designation they gave you. I guess you can't all go around calling each other 'Lisa' all the time. That would get confusing."

She walked around the two Widows, watching their muscles tense, their breathing, heartrate, assessing all their reactions.

"Not that it matters. A93 and…" Jessica said, then waited for the other Widow to speak. "No? Not going to offer up your digits? Oh well, you'll still be Number Two in my records then. Unfortunate. You seem to be the one who was less…crazy."

A93's lips curled into a sneer. "Let me out of this field and I'll show you crazy."

Jessica held up a hand and splayed her fingers wide. Tendrils of energy arced between her fingers, running along the superconductor lines within her skin. "You didn't see this, what with our resident ancient man kicking your ass, A93, but your friend Number Two did. If you were to 'show me crazy', I think it would just end up with me cooking that pasty white skin of yours."

A93 pursed her lips, and Jessica suspected she would have ground her teeth—had she any to grind.

"I suppose I'll just go, then," Jessica said after a minute. "You're not really that interesting, and given that you jumped the gun, we have more than enough time to get out of here. We're so deep in the retro-zone anyway, that I doubt we need to worry about any help coming your way."

The moment she said those words, Jessica activated the stasis field and froze the two Widows in place.

A93's mouth was open, and the other, likely more stable of the two, was glaring at her.

<*What do you think she's about to say?*> Iris asked.

"Something about how we're going to get it," Jessica replied as she stepped up to the other Widow and looked in her eyes.

<*Her vitals spiked right before you snapped on the field.*>

Jessica nodded. "I noticed that."

She walked behind the two women and deactivated the stasis field, watching their expressions through the room's cameras.

"You wait and see!" A93 said while the other Widow shouted, "Shut up!"

Then they realized Jessica was gone and A93 turned her head as much as the field would allow and glared at Number Two. "*You* shut up. We had the perfect chance to grab the ship and you wanted to get whoever came for the bait."

"Shuuut up," Number Two growled.

"If you'd been here, we'd have Finaeus and the ship and could take it to Costa."

"They have cameras…audio pickup," the other Widow said. "They're going to hear this!"

"I don't care anymore," A93 said. "I had him. I had Finaeus. If you were there—"

"Finaeus isn't the primary target. He's not even secondary. The ship, and Jessica. If you'd been in position we'd have Jessica and then we would have taken the ship as well."

Jessica had always found it interesting how people would talk more if there wasn't a human present—even if they knew they were being recorded.

A decent operative would have stayed quiet regardless, but it seemed A93 *was* losing it, and the other woman was desperate to keep her companion quiet.

"And Jessica would have come back to the ship if we had it!" A93 shouted. "We could have taken her then."

Number Two didn't respond, and both of the Widows glared at each other, their rage-filled expressions a perfect mirror of one another.

"Costa, you say?" Jessica asked as she walked around the two. "An Orion Guard base, right? I suppose it makes sense that there are bases in the retro-zone—what with us being so close to the Inner Stars and all. But I wonder…would you take our ship to just any base?"

After the initial expressions of shock dissipated, the two Widows only stared mutely at Jessica.

"No matter," Jessica replied with a wave of her hand. "This was just the warmup."

She walked back to her seat and sat down once more, looking from one Widow to the other and back again. "You two clones are clearly losing it. Proximity to such a strong reminder of your old life has done a number on you. You knew that Finaeus married again, right? More than once too. I wonder if he never managed to quite replace you. I met one of his daughters. Now *that* was an impressive woman.

"You two husks? Not so much."

A93 drew in a sharp breath, but didn't reply. Jessica saw tears form in her eyes and knew she could push harder and get more, but suddenly she didn't have the stomach for it. She felt more pity than anger when she looked at the two human wrecks before her.

Jessica snapped the stasis field into place and left the room, taking the chair with her. They had enough to start with for now. If the Widows' ship and 'Costa' didn't pan out, she'd have another go.

<I'm surprised,> Iris commented as Jessica stopped and leant against a bulkhead. *<I thought you'd push them harder.>*

<I should have,> Jessica replied. *<It's just…those two didn't ask to get made.>*

<No one asks to get made,> Iris countered. *<We're all born out of our parent's hubris. Well, AIs are at least. You humans are born out of a lot of chemicals and grunting.>*

Jessica laughed and shook her head. *<Usually some hubris in there too. Either way, they're different. I don't think life has presented them with many great choices.>*

Iris sighed. *<I suppose you're right. Still, if they'd hurt Piya and Cheeky…>*

<Well, yeah, then I'd have torn their creepy white skin right off 'til I got what I needed.>

<Good.>

SHIPNAPPING

STELLAR DATE: 03.12.8948 (Adjusted Years)
LOCATION: Yessen, Ur, Sullus System
REGION: Midway Cluster, Orion Freedom Alliance Space

Jessica stood near the edge of the wide concourse running through Wing 9 of Yessen.

Rock walls rose up at the edges of the wing, arching into vaulted ceiling high overhead. Every few hundred meters, large doors were set into the stone walls, leading into the bays on either side of the wing.

<*Funny that they've named this one '9',*> Jessica commented to Iris. <*There are only four wings. They're not even in a pattern. I could see numbering them 3, 5, 7, 9 or something like that, but its 1, 4, 7, 9. It makes no sense.*>

<*Entries in the city's databases claim that they planned on making more, but ran out of money,*> Iris replied.

<*Then why not renumber them?*>

<*Should I see if any of Yessen's original city planners are still around?*> Iris asked with a mental smirk. <*You could ask them and not me.*>

<*Funny girl,*> Jessica replied. <*Have you made your way into the bay's records yet?*>

<*In, yes. I'm now altering their data to show you as the owner of the* Sierra Echo.>

Jessica wondered if the name had special meaning for the Widows, or if it had just been the designation their ship had been given when it had rolled off the line.

She looked across Wing 9's main thoroughfare and into Bay 91A. She could see the *Sierra Echo* on a pad on the far side. There were half a dozen ships visible in all, and more cargo than she'd ever let sit unguarded in a bay, but things ran fast and loose in Yessen. Barely good enough seemed to be just right.

On the way to Ur they'd debated a dozen ways to take the Widows' ship. Everything from masquerading as one of the creepy assassins to pretending they were a repo crew.

None of the women were the right height or physique to pull off a Widow, and it was probable that someone in a position of authority knew the *Sierra Echo* was a government vessel.

So it fell to Jessica—or more accurately, Iris—to get them onto the ship.

Jessica was just the ride.

<*OK, you're golden. I've altered all their feeds to show you and one of the Widows coming off the ship when it arrived. Your tokens now register you as the owner. All the* Sierra Echo's *fees are paid for. Filing for takeoff clearance now.*>

<*You're the best, Iris. I mean that literally too. You're actually the best.*>

Iris laughed. <*And don't I know it!*>

Before she could move, Trevor's voice broke into her thoughts. <*I just dropped off Hunter's crate at the warehouse. I'll be back on the* Sexy *in ten minutes, and back up to Sabrina in thirty.*>

<*Don't get in any trouble before we meet at the rendezvous,*> Jessica admonished with a wink and a grin.

<*I live for trouble,*> Trevor replied.

<*Isn't that my line?*>

<*Maybe. Just be careful, Jessica.*>

Jessica snorted. *<Trevor, it's me.>*

<Exactly. See you soon.>

<OK, here goes nothing,> Jessica said as she walked across the concourse and into Bay 91A.

It was Yessen's first shift, the bay thrummed with activity as loaders shuffled cargo in and out of ships. A dozen crew sauntered off a shuttle on her right, laughing loudly and daring one another to acts of general stupidity for their shore leave.

Jessica walked through their midst as though she owned the place and noted with satisfaction that several of the men and women turned to give her appreciative looks.

<Always such a showoff,> Iris chided.

<Best way to allay suspicion is to behave like you're trying to attract attention.>

<You sure are good at that.>

Jessica laughed. *<I certainly am. And I make a fine meatsuit to haul your ship-hacking mind around in.>*

<Awww, Jessica, you're more than my meat suit. I'm not sure what more, but certainly something.>

<You're all heart, Iris. Which is impressive considering that you have no heart.>

Jessica released a passel of nano into the air as they approached the ship and slowed her pace to give Iris time to access the vessel's airlock panel and security systems.

After a few moments, Iris reported in. *<As expected, this is an order of magnitude better than any of the tech we've hit in the retro-zone. Better than anything since we jumped into Perseus—barring Star City, of course.>*

<I'll do a walkabout, then,> Jessica replied and changed her approach, angling toward the *Sierra Echo*'s bow.

It was a good looking vessel, thin and long, its hull an interesting configuration comprised of overlapping plates. Unless Jessica missed her guess, those plates could shift positions to alter the ship's profile to appear larger or smaller on scan as needed. Not a lot, but enough to fool many non-military scan systems.

She walked underneath the vessel's bow and checked over the scan fin, and the mount points on which the ship rested. It was the sort of walkthrough a fastidious owner would make when they didn't trust that their ship had been taken care of.

"I hope it's to your—oh, sorry, I thought you were someone else."

Jessica turned and eyed the speaker, an older woman of middling height who wore the uniform of a Yessen spaceport worker.

"Is she fueled up?" Jessica asked with an arched eyebrow. "I want to be on my way as soon as we're cleared for departure."

"Umm…yes, but who are you?"

"Jessica," she said, turning her gaze back to the ship's hull.

"Jessica, that's great, but I spoke with the two women who came off this ship the other day. I got the distinct impression that the *Sierra Echo* belonged to them."

Jessica turned back to the woman, staring down her nose. "Well, your impression was wrong. Check your records. This is my ship, and I'll be leaving in it shortly."

The woman pulled out a pad, a rather quaint affectation, and scowled as she looked it over. "Huh," she eventually replied. "Ship does appear to be yours. There's even a record of you disembarking…funny, I was on duty then. I'm certain I would have remembered you."

<I have access to the airlock,> Iris said to Jessica. *<Get up there and we'll end this silly debate.>*

<Gladly.>

"Well, if she's fueled up, get that umbilical detached so I can get out of this shit-hole," Jessica said as she walked out from under the ship, brushing past the woman.

"Don't have to be so rude about it," the woman muttered.

She followed Jessica out and watched intently as Jessica climbed the ramp and stood before the airlock door.

<Umm…Iris, I passed the codes, why's the door not opening. It's not in a lockdown or anything.>

<I can see that. Just a second,> Iris replied, her voice rushed.

"Need a hand?" the woman asked from the base of the ramp. "Funny how you can't get the door open on your own ship."

Jessica glanced over her shoulder and called back. "I'm reviewing the security measures to ensure that no one messed with my girl. Do you have anything to worry about?"

Beyond the woman, Jessica spotted a pair of security guards enter the bay and begin walking toward her.

<*Shit! That woman called security on us!*> Jessica exclaimed. <*This is going to get real awkward real fast.*>

Jessica turned back toward the ship, trying to act as relaxed as possible, while considering the exits and egress routes. Taking out the guards wouldn't be too tricky, but the bay had defense turrets at the exits. Those would be trickier.

Then the *Sierra Echo*'s airlock cycled open and Jessica calmly stepped in.

<*Were you actually worried?*> Iris asked.

<*Well, you sounded concerned, so I was too.*>

<*Ye of little faith.*>

Jessica cycled the airlock's inner door and stepped into the vessel's main compartment. The room was as spare and utilitarian as the Widows themselves. It sported an armory, a pair of stasis pods, a small kitchenette, and four bunks.

"Four bunks," Jessica said to herself as she walked past them toward the cockpit.

<*Noticed that too. They're all perfectly made, can't tell which were in use.*>

"I kinda imagined the Widows sleeping in coffins."

<*Seems fitting.*>

The cockpit was a standard four-seat arrangement, and Jessica slid into one of the seats.

<*She's in standby, bringing her back up,*> Iris said. <*Their initialization protocols are weird, though. I wonder if we should have extracted the command codes from the widows.*>

Jessica sighed. <*Yeah, we probably should have. They're just so….*>

<*Gross?*>

<Pathetic.>

Jessica pulled her feeds from the nano in the bay and spotted the two guards talking to the woman, who was gesturing at the *Sierra Echo.* One of the guards shook his head and then they both walked away.

"Take that, you nosy Nancy," Jessica said. "Of course…she was right, we are stealing the ship, but still."

A minute later the console came alive, and Iris passed the ship's new command tokens to Jessica.

<What a pain. There was an NSAI aboard that was really not happy to have us.>

"Things often take you a minute or two, this was faster. How was that a pain?"

Iris made a harrumph sound before responding. *<Normally things here in the retro-zone take that long because of how ancient and slow their networking protocols are. Seriously, people used better stuff before the Sentience Wars in some cases.* ***This*** *was slow because that thing kept blocking ports and shutting down every system I wormed my way into. It was slow because it was fast.>*

"I can't wait to get back to civilization."

<Tell me about it.>

Jessica initialized a pre-flight check and made a call into the station to get the umbilicals—which were still connected to the ship—detached.

The ship's checks all came up green, and Jessica looked up the docking bay's departure queue. They were the only one in the bay in the queue, though three adjacent bays had ships ahead of them. ETA for lift-off was seven minutes.

Provided the umbilicals were pulled off.

"I have half a mind to go out there and do it myself," Jessica muttered. "That woman is obviously stalling it just to be an ass."

<Maybe you should call in to the station master.>

"Nah, that'll take just as long to get through to someone who gives a shit."

Jessica rose from the seat and walked out of the cockpit, through the ship's main room. The inner door on the airlock was closed—as it should be, the pre-flight process closed both doors. But for just a moment, it looked like the outside door was cycling shut.

A quick check of the ship's systems indicated the door had not been open, and Jessica assumed it must have just been a trick of the light.

Jessica palmed the inner airlock door open at the exact moment she realized none of her nano within the airlock were responding.

Iris must have noticed as well, because she cried out, *<Duck!>* right as the door opened.

Jessica was already diving to the side, but not fast enough to avoid being clipped by a pulse shot rippling out of the open airlock.

She pulled her own pistol from its holster and fired into the airlock while taking cover behind the kitchenette's counter.

"That you, Lisa?" Jessica called out. "Thought no one was home. I could put on some tea."

"Who's Lisa?" a voice said from within the airlock. "I'm A103."

"OK, A103, do *you* want some tea?"

A shape darted out of the airlock, and Jessica fired on it, but missed as the misty figure took cover behind the stasis pods.

She could tell the Widow was making her way toward the armory where several rifles rested in a rack, two with charge cylinders attached.

<Those are going to be biolocked for sure,> Jessica said to Iris.

<Yeah, and I don't have enough free nano at the moment to unlock those weapons before she does.>

Jessica sighed. Then they'd do this the old-fashioned way.

She crouched low and drew in a deep breath before she leapt from her cover and sprinted across the small space. The Widow rose up from behind the stasis pod and fired her pistol, but Jessica held out her hands and nullified the wave.

Betcha didn't see that coming, you poor messed up little woman....

Jessica dove over the pod, reaching for the woman's neck. The Widow was fast and darted to the side, but Jessica slammed a hand down on the surface of the stasis pod and pivoted midair.

Her shin slammed into the Widow's helmet, knocking the woman to the ground, while sending a sharp pain up Jessica's leg.

Jessica twisted midair and landed in a crouch between the pods, watching as the Widow flipped backward also landing on her feet.

"Nice moves," Jessica said. "Did Finaeus teach them to you?"

The Widow cocked her head. "Finaeus?"

Jessica wondered if the two Widows they'd captured on Ferra had told A103 about Finaeus's presence on the ship. Surely this one had to have known before they got to the Sullus System.

<*I wonder if it had been in the stasis pods until recently…maybe the other two went rogue and locked this one down,*> Iris suggested.

<*Then who let it out?*>

Jessica didn't have time for further conversation as the Widow fired her pulse pistol again. Another counter-wave nullified the pulse weapon's concussive wave, and her Retyna gauge now showed very little charge was left in her microbes.

Discharging in Parda City to hide her glow, plus the battle with the other Widow on the Peerless Transport ship had taken much of her energy.

<*You should have slept in the upper lounge. It had full sunlight the whole way from Ferra to Ur.*>

<*If wishes were fishes,*> Jessica responded as she returned fire at the Widow. One of the shots clipped the Widow in the shoulder and spun her around, knocking the slim woman over the last stasis pod.

Landing her right next to the armory.

<*Well played,*> Iris said, her voice dripping with sarcasm

<*Thanks, Iris. Is internal a-grav online?*>

Jessica didn't wait for Iris to respond before leaping into the air. Luckily, Iris knew what she was thinking—or close enough.

The moment Jessica was in the air, Iris activated a reverse a-grav field inside the ship. Making it a zero-*g* environment.

The Widow had grabbed a rifle and pulled it out of the rack at the exact moment gravity disappeared. The motion sent her spinning—right into Jessica's fists.

The Widow grunted, and the two would have separated once more, but Jessica managed to get an arm around the woman's neck.

She tried to deliver a dose of nano into the Widow's armor, but countermeasures stopped her attack cold.

The two women floated through the ship's central room, grappling with one another and landing blows where they could. Jessica took an armored fist to the head, and then another to the stomach. The Widow managed to get her arms around Jessica's neck and pulled back hard.

Jessica gasped for breath as the Widow's motion sent them spinning.

<*Iris!*> Jessica thought desperately.

<*Wait three, two, one!*>

The a-grav systems reversed, generating over five gravities of acceleration within the ship.

Jessica slammed to the ground, directly atop the Widow. An instant later, gravity reverted to normal, and Jessica rolled away, looking back at her enemy to see the woman's neck bent at an unnatural angle and her body twitching.

Jessica rolled her own neck, keenly aware of how close she'd come to being the one in that condition.

<*Nice move,*> she said to Iris, not ready to hear what her throat sounded like after nearly choking to death.

<*I'll admit, I was worried at the last moment. There was a thirty percent chance she'd shift and both your necks would be broken.*>

<*Yay for statistics,*> Jessica replied as she walked to the closest stasis pod and hit the big green 'open' button. Once the lid was up, she strode back to the Widow. <*Can you give me a half-*g *off?*>

<*Sure,*> Iris replied, and Jessica felt her body become considerably lighter. She reached down and scooped up the Widow. <*She may not survive, even with stasis.*>

<*Less worried about her survival, and more making sure she doesn't somehow come back to life and kill me while I'm flying this thing.*>

<*That's a strange paranoia,*> Iris replied. <*On the plus side, the bay has disconnected the umbilicals. We're good to go.*>

Jessica walked to the kitchenette and grabbed a water pouch before returning to the cockpit. <*What about that woman out there. She wasn't the Widow in disguise, was she?*>

<*She's still standing out there. Arguing with someone new. We're t-minus thirty seconds.*>

Jessica settled into her seat and sucked on the water pouch. "Too late now, Nosey Nancy."

She powered up the ship's grav drives and signaled the bay to release the locks on the docking cradle. The locks released, and the *Sierra Echo* floated into the air above the cradle.

The bay's exit extended upward—through a kilometer shaft carved into the rock—and Jessica eased the vessel up and above Ur's surface. She glanced down at the structures around the space port, and at Yessen's top-side dome a few kilometers distant.

"So long, Ur. Thanks for the ship," Jessica said as she increased the drive's thrust and angled the ship to stay in her breakaway lane.

<Your throat must be feeling better,> Iris commented.

"The water helped," Jessica replied as she located *Sabrina* in the traffic patterns above Ur and sent a tightbeam message: "We had another skinny black visitor, but we're free and clear. Meet you at the rendezvous."

A moment later a response came back from Cargo. "Glad to hear it. See you in a week."

It took several more hours to guide the ship through the traffic lanes and onto an outsystem vector. It would be two days to the FTL jump point, and then three more to the rendezvous location the crew had selected.

"More than enough time for a nap," Jessica said as she peeled off her shipsuit and reclined her seat. "Stars are dim here, but some light is better than no light."

<Once we reach out max v *I'll spin the ship to give you some light from Sullus.>*

"You're a peach," Jessica said as she closed her eyes and let her first sleep in two days overtake her.

DESTINATION: COSTA

STELLAR DATE: 03.18.8948 (Adjusted Years)
LOCATION: Interstellar Space, 2ly from the Sullus System
REGION: Midway Cluster, Orion Freedom Alliance Space

Sabrina and the *Sierra Echo* dropped out of FTL within a million kilometers of each other, and once the ships were within a hundred milliseconds of comm lag, Jessica and Iris joined the crew on *Sabrina's* bridge via holodisplay.

"So, what's the word?" Cargo asked.

Jessica couldn't help but let a wide grin grow across her face. "We may have learned something."

"What kind of something?" Cheeky asked, a frown marring her delicate features. "You have surprise-face."

"I do, don't I?" Jessica chuckled. "Costa is an Orion Guard military base. It's not a major installation, looks like a patrol stopover in a system near here. The Quera System, to be precise."

"Huh," Cargo grunted. "Local maps don't have anything in Quera. Just few old mining outposts that shut down years ago."

"Well, the OG has an installation out there, and that's where the Widows were going to take us and *Sabrina*."

"Why?" Finaeus asked. "It's four light years closer to the Inner Stars, away from their major installations."

Jessica winked at Finaeus. "Oh, I don't know. Maybe because Costa has a jump gate."

Finaeus let out a whoop. "Well, hot-diggity-damn. We get to take a short cut home after all!"

"Or to the Andromeda Galaxy," Cheeky said. "I don't know that I want to chance another jump gate."

"Hey, whoa. That was a one-in-a-million thing. This time we'll do better. Besides, this solves our problem of how to get out of Orion space now that they know we're here."

"*Do* they know we're here?" Trevor asked Jessica. "Had the Widows reported in about us?"

Jessica nodded, still grinning. "Yes, but that's the best part. Our friends down in Hold 7 jumped the gun alright. Costa sent almost its entire fleet to the Sullus System—it'll be arriving there tomorrow. The station is pretty much empty."

<*This seems almost too good to be true,*> Sabrina said.

"Yeah, seriously?" Nance asked. "So, there's a jump gate, at an out of the way system—which sounds a bit familiar—but this time there's no massive fleet protecting it?"

"Yeah," Jessica continued to grin at her crewmates. "Looks like there will be just a few patrol vessels. The gate orbits a small moon that in turn orbits a mars-sized planet. There's an outpost down on the planet, and another on the moon—which is more like an asteroid. Either way, I think we can get in, hack the gate controls, and then hop on home."

As Jessica spoke, she watched the faces of the crew. They all appeared to be optimistic—by varying degrees. Cheeky looked the most uncertain, which wasn't surprising given what she'd gone through the last time they'd hijacked a jump gate.

"Gate control will be on that asteroid-moon, then," Finaeus said. "We'll need to get on there, take control of it, and then make our jump."

"Except we won't have your daughter helping us this time," Cargo said.

"And we won't have a Grey Division colonel trying to kill us," Finaeus countered. "Look, it's not going to be easy, but we have a way in."

"Which is?" Cheeky asked.

"This ship," Jessica said. "We just need some Widows to crew it. Who's up for that?"

Cheeky snorted. "Not me. That outfit they wear is way too constricting."

"Plus your breasts won't fit," Finaeus said with a grin.

"If we do this, we'll need three Widows." Cargo glanced at Jessica's holoimage. "It was just the three, right? One didn't get left behind on Ferra or Ur?"

Jessica nodded. "Just the three, yes. I'm out of the running. They're shorter than I am. A lot shorter. Nance, Cheeky, it'll have to be you two plus Addie."

"Seriously?" Cheeky asked. "Are you really volunteering me for this? I don't want to get on that ship, fly into some other system, pretend to be an evil Widow bitch, and infiltrate a station."

"I'm not keen on that either," Finaeus added.

"Don't forget the surgery we'll need to do," Nance said with a long sigh. "I agree, though. It's the best way. Plus, we'll finally get to New Canaan. It'll shave a decade off the trip. That's worth a tight outfit for a few hours."

"And we'll pull out all the stops," Cargo added. "No more hiding and skulking. Once the gate is under our control, we hit hard with everything we have."

"Wait, Nance!" Cheeky exclaimed. "What are you talking about, surgery?"

"The Widows are clones," Nance explained. "That means they're identical. Addie's an AHAP, so she can match them. You and I, however are shaped a bit differently."

"They are *slightly* different heights," Finaeus added. "Clones aren't always perfectly identical. We'll need to match each of you to the Widow closest to you."

Cheeky looked to Jessica. "Are you sure about this? Is there no other plan?"

"It's infiltration, or full-frontal assault," Jessica replied. "I'm open to other options. We don't always need to use my first plan."

Everyone looked around the room at each other crewmember for a minute before Cheeky spoke up.

"Well, someone's going to need to make those helmets bigger. I'm not letting you slice off my nose!"

THE NEW WIDOWS

STELLAR DATE: 03.20.8948 (Adjusted Years)
LOCATION: *Sabrina*, Dark Layer
REGION: Midway Cluster, Orion Freedom Alliance Space

<They're awake,> Finaeus called up from the medbay. *<They should be dressed and ready in fifteen minutes.>*

<'Kay, let us know when to come see them,> Jessica replied as she took a sip of her coffee while staring over the cup's rim at Trevor.

"I know what you're thinking," Trevor said. "It's a good plan. It'll work."

"I…" Jessica shook her head. "I sure hope so. Cheeky's really not ready for this."

"She can handle it." Trevor reached across the table and took Jessica's hand. "She's been through worse. Besides, you'll be with them the whole time."

"Well, not all of them all the time," Jessica said. "They're going to turn me over to someone. Probably the base commander."

"See, now that's the part I really don't like," Trevor replied. "The part where you're all alone in a stasis pod."

Jessica tapped her head and grinned. "I'm never alone."

<Galaxy's most bad-ass infiltration specialist at your service,> Iris chimed in. *<Truth be told, with six of us girls in there, those Oggies won't know what hit em.>*

"Isn't it seven?" Trevor asked.

<Erin, Piya, me, Jessica, Cheeky, and Nance. Adds up to six to me,> Iris replied.

Trevor 's brow creased. "What about Addie?"

<Addie's not a person, Trevor. She's a thing. Like a gun, or a toaster oven. I don't count the guns we bring along.>

"But she's combat effective," Trevor pushed. "I think Addie's more than just an NSAI."

"Let's call it six and a half," Jessica offered.

"OK, six and a half."

Jessica winked at Trevor and took another sip of her coffee. "This is going to work. It won't be a cakewalk, but it'll work."

"Let's go over the plan one more time—for my sake," Trevor said bringing up the station's schematics over the table. "OK, here's Costa. The station's command center is here, and they'll probably tuck your stasis pod here."

As Trevor spoke, two points lit up on the station, showing the secure storage as two levels and three hundred meters from the command center.

"Right. We'll secret a weapon or two—or three—into the pod, plus our last hackit. I'll get out of the pod—not sure how we'll fake stasis, but Finaeus seems to think he can—and meet up with our Widows. We'll set the hackit loose on one route and take another to the command center."

Two routes highlighted on the station's schematics.

"With luck," Jessica continued, "One or two of our Widows will be there already—or at least close by. We take control of the station from their command center, and you pick us up in the *Sexy* at this airlock here."

"And your auxiliary egress is back on the Widow's ship," Trevor added.

"Yeah, we're going to see if Cheeky can stay close to it and get back aboard. It would be a great prize to bring to New Canaan with us."

A rueful laugh escaped Trevor's lips. "You're always thinking strategically."

Jessica leant forward. "There's a war brewing between Orion and the Transcend. Not this cold war that's been going on forever, either. A real war. Any intel we bring back will be critical."

"You think that your Tanis Richards will let New Canaan be drawn into the conflict?"

"Honestly? I think New Canaan will be at the *heart* of the conflict."

* * * * *

Addie stood outside the medbay, already wearing the Widow's armor and helmet. The sight of her gave Jessica a small chill. She'd fought two Widows so far, and neither had been easy or fun.

"Hi, Addie," Jessica said, trying to dispel her unease.

"Who? I'm A93," Addie replied.

"Don't assume personality yet," Jessica said. "Not until I tell you."

Addie relaxed, changing her posture before nodding. "Understood, Jessica,"

As the AHAP spoke, the medbay door opened and Nance and Cheeky walked out, also wearing the black armor of the Widows, but both still carrying their helmets.

"This is freaking weird," Cheeky said, looking down at herself. "My boobs are so small! Nance, how do you go through life with tiny tits like this?"

Nance rolled her eyes. "With less back strain than you, that's how."

Jessica looked the pair over and nodded with satisfaction. The Widows were lithe and thin, very close to Nance's physique, but they were a few centimeters shorter. Finaeus had shaved those centimeters off Nance in a variety of places, shrinking her down to Widow height.

Cheeky, on the other hand, was shorter than the Widows, and curvier. Her body was stretched and slimmed out. While Nance looked close to her prior self, Cheeky looked like her head had been grafted onto a different body.

"When you brought this plan up, I knew I'd hate this," Cheeky said, glaring at Jessica. "Guess what? I hate it."

Finaeus walked out of the medbay and wrapped an arm around Cheeky. "Don't worry. I hate it too and I'll make you your Cheeky self again first once this is done."

Cheeky turned and wagged a finger in Finaeus's face. "You'd better. I don't want to be this skinny thing any longer than I have to."

<You're still the same on the inside, that's what counts,> Piya added. *<Nothing about how you look can change your cheekiness.>*

Cheeky craned her neck, looking back at her butt. "I don't know about that. I don't feel particularly Cheeky right now."

"Jessica," Finaeus said, turning from Cheeky. "I've modified the stasis pod you'll be using on the *Sierra Echo.* It has the hackit, some weapons, a satchel of explosives, and a tactical helmet if you want it."

"Won't people know she's not in stasis?" Cheeky asked. "She'll be breathing and stuff."

Finaeus shook his head. "All stasis pods use holodisplays to show the person inside. You actually can't see into stasis, it's just a feel-good thing."

"Really?" Cheeky asked, then nodded slowly. "Oh…I guess that makes sense, how can photons reflect off matter if it's in a state of stasis. Never thought of that before."

Finaeus lifted a finger in the air and proclaimed, "Science!"

"Put your helmets on," Jessica directed. "I want to see if the final result is as freakin' creepy as I think it's going to be."

Nance and Cheeky put their helmets on and Trevor laughed. "Yup, creepy as can be."

Cheeky pulled her helmet off. "And a really tight fit too!"

"Sorry," Finaeus replied. I adjusted them as much as I can to let you keep your ears and noses. Either they get squished, or they have to go.

Cheeky reached up and touched her nose, glaring at Finaeus. "No chance! Took a lot of work to get this nose just right. You'd go and make it some big honker afterward."

"Easy," Finaeus said, raising his hands. "I'm not advocating that at all. It's why I altered the helmets."

"OK, ladies," Jessica said to the three new Widows. "Clock's ticking. We need to get over to the *Sierra Echo* and push off from *Sabrina*."

"You ready to fly solo, Sabs?" Cheeky asked.

<I am, I believe I found my gut. It's worried and nervous to have you leave again, but it's there.>

Cheeky laughed and patted the hull. "Don't worry, I'll be back before you know it."

Sabrina led the two women and the AHAP to the forward airlock where the *Sierra Echo* was docked. It felt strange not taking anything with them. No clothes, weapons, no gear of any sort. They had to make do with only what was on the Widows' ship.

Jessica stopped at the forward airlock and turned back to face Trevor.

"You be careful," he said, wrapping her in his tree-trunk arms. "Don't make me have to come in there and kick some ass to save you."

"I like watching you kick ass," Jessica said with a smirk. "But I've probably seen enough that I don't need to watch it again just yet. It's going to be a piece of cake. In, hack, out, jump. Just like that."

Trevor gave her a final squeeze. "Just like that."

They separated reluctantly, and Jessica tapped Cheeky on the shoulder—interrupting a rather noisy kiss with Finaeus. "C'mon Cheeks, you can suck face all you want when this is done."

"That's not all we'll be su—"

"Cheeky! Really?" Nance admonished.

Jessica chuckled, and Cheeky gave Finaeus a final peck on the cheek before walking past Nance and patting her on the head. "And you wonder why we call you 'Mom'."

They stepped into the airlock, cycled it and floated through the umbilical to the *Sierra Echo.* Once inside, Cheeky looked around and shook her head. "Feels so…sterile. I bet you like that, eh Nance?"

Nance looked around and shook her head. "There's sterility, and then there's lacking any sort of atmosphere whatsoever. This is a place where machines work, not people."

"I wonder how far off that is," Jessica replied.

"I think I resent that," Addie said.

Cheeky glanced at Addie. "Don't worry, Addie, you have plenty of personality."

"That's good, I'm programmed to."

<See?> Iris spoke up. *<NSAI.>*

"I wasn't arguing that point," Jessica replied as she walked into the cockpit. "Cheeky, why don't you do the honors."

Cheeky sat in the front-left seat and looked over the controls. "Pretty standard stuff for Orion-land."

"Yeah, not so different from the *Sexy*," Jessica replied.

<Except for the stealth systems,> Erin said. *<Not as good as the ones we got from the* Intrepid, *but rather impressive.>*

<Sabrina, *this is* Sierra Echo,> Cheeky called in. *<We're sealed up and good to go. Unlatching from umbilical.>*

<Ship-side clamps released,> Sabrina responded. *<Grav field ready for you to push off.>*

<Acknowledged,> Cheeky said. *<Pushing off in five, four, three, two, one…mark.>*

With no discernible feeling whatsoever, the two vessels began to move apart in the never-ending nothingness of the dark layer.

<*You ladies be careful out there,*> Cargo said. <*We'll be one hour behind you. Anything goes wrong—****anything****—and you call for evac. We'll smoke that base and make our way home the old-fashioned way. None of your lives are worth a jump.*>

<*Thanks, Dad,*> Cheeky said with a grin insufficient to hide her nervousness from Jessica. <*We'll be careful and be back before curfew.*>

<*See that you are,*> Cargo replied. <Sabrina *out.*>

<*You got it.* Sierra Echo, *out.*>

COSTA

STELLAR DATE: 03.22.8948 (Adjusted Years)
LOCATION: Approaching Costa Station, Quera System
REGION: Midway Cluster, Orion Freedom Alliance Space

"I have a bad feeling about this," Cheeky said as they slotted into their assigned approach lane for Costa Station.

Jessica patted Cheeky on the shoulder. "It's just nerves. We have a plan, it'll work."

"And if it doesn't, we'll improvise," Nance said with a soft laugh. "Like we always do when Jessica's initial plan doesn't work."

"Hey, I put the plan out there for everyone to iterate on. It's not my fault no one ever offers up their own suggestions."

Cheeky laughed. "That's your new callsign. You're Plan Girl."

"How come all my nicknames have girl in them?" Jessica asked. "First Retyna Girl, now this."

"Jessica?" Nance asked, and Jessica turned to see a mischievous grin on the woman's face. "I think you're forgetting 'J-Doll' from back on Chittering Hawk."

"Stars…I've been trying to scrub that from my memory."

"J-Doll and Trevor the Annihilator in a c-c-c-caaaage match," Cheeky intoned.

Jessica couldn't help but laugh at Cheeky's impression of the announcer's voice. "I don't think they called him Trevor the Annihilator."

"So what did they call him?" Cheeky asked.

Jessica tried to think back, but the memories were hazy. It wasn't an event she liked to dwell on. "I have no idea, I was glaring at Camilla at the time, wishing that she'd burst into flame."

<*It was 'The Mountain',*> Iris supplied. <*And the announcer stuttered the 'M'. The M-m-m-m-mooooouuuuntain!*>

"Huh," Cheeky said with a furrowed brow. "We call him 'Mountain Man' all the time. I wonder if it bothers him."

Jessica wondered the same thing. She hoped it didn't; she'd called him that a lot over the years.

<*If it had bothered him, he'd have mentioned it,*> Iris said privately. <*Trevor's not one to hide how he feels about things, or let them fester.*>

<*Good point, Mountain Man he shall remain.*>

The three women chatted idly for the final two hours of their approach into Costa station. Jessica watched the station grow from a single point of light passing around the planet Albis to an oblong rock, a little more than one hundred kilometers in length.

A large docking ring wrapped around the asteroid-moon, and parts of the station protruded from the grey surface as though they were trying to burst free from the rock.

The structure was reminiscent of Vesta, one of the larger asteroids in Sol's asteroid belt. Jessica had never been there, but Tanis had regaled her with several tales of the days she had been stationed there.

It was where Tanis had received her first AI, if Jessica remembered correctly.

Beyond Costa, lazily drifting around the station, was the jump gate.

It was much smaller than the gate at Grey Wolf, but larger than the one the RHY Dynamics ships had used in the Perry System.

Two small patrol craft drifted near the gate and another pair were visible on the other side of the station. Scan showed another dozen patrol ships, and one destroyer-class vessel docked on Costa's ring. Otherwise, the system appeared to be entirely devoid of human activity.

"I guess I'd better go get in my pod," Jessica said as she rose from her seat and walked back into the ship's central room.

"Don't want to watch final approach?" Cheeky asked.

"I don't want them to see me through the front window on this ship," Jessica replied as she selected the command to open the pod.

Nance stood and approached Jessica. "I'll tuck you in all snug."

Jessica laughed and then winked at Nance. "Thanks, Mom."

"Dammit!"

Jessica climbed into the pod and lay down, calling out before the lid closed. "Oh, and you two! Get your helmets on. If they see your smiling faces through the cockpit window, we'll be onto plan B in no time."

<*What's plan B, again?*> Piya asked.

<*Shoot our way through the whole damn station,*> Jessica replied.

The pod sealed shut, and Jessica tapped into the ship's systems, watching the final approach. The station had assigned them an internal berth within the station proper, not out on the docking ring.

The station's acting commanding officer, a colonel named Ortaga sent a greeting and informed the Widows that he would meet them at the dock.

As the *Sierra Echo* passed into its bay and settled into a cradle, Jessica found herself holding her breath. It would all be on Nance now.

* * * * *

Nance settled her helmet into place, grimacing at how it squished her nose.

<*Remember,*> Erin said. <*You're A103. You're a Widow, a cold-hearted killing machine. You don't answer to Colonel Ortaga, you're just stopping here and transferring the prisoner while you wait for the fleet to return with their other prize,* Sabrina.>

Nance nodded. <*Yes. I'm an evil bitch whose bitter after being subjected to years of Finaeus's terrible humor. These people won't know what hit them.*>

<*Try to be serious, Nance.*>

<*It'll all be serious soon enough.*>

Addie approached Nance. "A103," Addie said in the creepy ethereal voice of the Widows. "Ready to disembark."

"Good," Nance replied. "Remember, A93. You stay with the pod and ensure Jessica has a safe exit. She'll direct you from there."

"I understand the mission," Addie replied in her normal voice. "You forget, this is my main reason for existing."

Nance nodded slowly. "Sorry, Addie. You're just eerily good at it."

"I'll consider that to be a compliment," Addie replied.

A vibration ran through the deck beneath their feet as the ship settled into the docking cradle and the inner airlock door cycled open.

"Good luck out there," Cheeky called from the cockpit where they'd decided she'd remain unless needed.

"Stay safe, Cheeks," Nance called back.

Nance stepped into the airlock first, and Addie followed, pushing the stasis pod forward on its hover pad. The outer lock cycled open and Nance walked down the ramp toward the colonel who waited at its end.

"Widows A103, A93," Colonel Ortaga said by way of greeting. "Welcome back to Costa, though I must admit I'm surprised to see you back so soon. Where is the ship you were after?"

"We were unable to secure it, but the fleet is in pursuit," Nance said, the helmet altering her voice to the breathy tones of a Widow. "We did, however, capture Jessica Keller."

"Keller? I'm not familiar with her," Colonel Ortaga said, his brow lowering.

"No. Chances are you wouldn't be," Nance replied. "However, she is one of Tanis Richard's closest confidants. There is much she may know about their technology, and plans."

"So the ship?" the colonel asked.

Nance guessed at the gist of his question and nodded in response. "It was the *Sabrina*, yes."

Colonel Ortaga shook his head in disbelief. "And it was out at Naga…how?"

"Jump gate, of course," Nance replied tersely. "Are we going to stand here all day, or shall we secure this stasis pod. When the fleet comes back with their ship, we'll need to send her through the gate."

Colonel Ortaga approached the pod and peered in. "Jessica Keller, you say. She's very…purple."

"I'd noticed," Nance replied, allowing more annoyance to fill her voice.

The colonel glanced up at Nance and seemed to pale slightly, then he looked back at Addie. "We could send her through now. I could have a ship readied."

Nance shook her head. "No, this is one of the greatest prizes we've ever captured. I'll not send her off on some courier."

<Well done, very forceful,> Erin said privately.

<Thanks Erin, I'm just channeling my inner mom.>

"Yes, of course. Follow me, we'll make sure she's secure."

They began to walk across the bay when Ortaga looked over his shoulder back at the *Sierra Echo*. "Where's A45?"

"She's attending to business." Nance replied without hesitation.

"Really?" Ortaga asked. "What sort of business?"

<He's pushy,> Erin commented.

Nance didn't turn her head. "Widow's business."

"What—"

She bit her lip, this man had to realize he couldn't question her, and realize it fast.

Nance took a quick step ahead of Ortaga, spun and put a hand on his chest. "Colonel. You do not have clearance for all our operations. If I tell you she is attending to Widow's business, you will take that as all of the answer you need."

<Dropping the hackit out of the pod now,> Erin said. *<Thanks for the distraction.>*

<Any time.>

Though the colonel was forty centimeters taller than Nance, he swallowed and nodded quickly.

Nance wondered how much of his reaction was because of the Widow's voice. To her it sounded like she was speaking from beyond the grave.

<It creeps me out too,> Erin said. *<I wonder if that's half the reason they talk like that.>*

<Intimidation is a powerful tool,> Nance replied.

Nance stood with her hand on the colonel's chest for a moment longer and then nodded. "Good. Lead on."

<OK…I kinda like this,> Nance said to Erin. *<When this is all said and done, I'm keeping the outfit.>*

<Stars…is it going to be your new hazsuit? Imagine what inspection teams will think of you when they come on board.>

<*What inspection teams?*> Nance asked. <*If this all goes well, it'll be our last time docking in a system we don't trust. The mission will be over.*>

<*You're not going to stay with* Sabrina?> Erin asked as they silently followed Colonel Ortaga through the station.

<*I'm not sure. But even if we do, will* Sabrina *continue to be a starfreighter?*> Nance asked. <*Hell, I don't even know what that means anymore. How could we go back to hauling crap from system to system with what we've seen?*>

<*I don't know…*> Erin began and then stopped. <*You know what will happen when we get back, right?*>

Nance bit her lip. She knew. She knew, and it terrified her. Erin was the one who kept her sane. Without Erin in her head, would the remnant just take over? Would it operate her like a puppet?

<*You'll leave me,*> Nance said after a minute's pause.

<*I'll stay as long as I can, but I'll get reassigned eventually. There's probably a lot to do at New Canaan. You know you're welcome to stay as well.*>

Nance knew that. She also knew the remnant had work for her in New Canaan. It would fall to her to hunt down the person who had infected her with Myrrdan's shard—or whatever it was.

The remnant would probably send her after Myrrdan as well.

It was the thing that drove her to support this plan of action. If not, she would have sided with Cheeky. Had that been the case, they may never have risked taking this jump gate.

There was one small hope in the back of Nance's mind: that when the *Intrepid*'s technicians removed Erin, they would see *something* that would alert them to the presence of the remnant.

And then they'd save her from it.

She tried to put it from her mind as they followed Colonel Ortaga through the base. The further in they went, the more deserted it seemed to be.

It made sense. The docking ring could support hundreds of ships, but there was only one destroyer in evidence. Either the entire fleet and all its support ships had left for the Sullus System, or Costa's use was in decline for some reason.

She looked up the station's records on the general network which revealed that—for the last century at least—Costa had never even reached full utilization.

<*Notice how the station is a ghost town?*> Nance asked Erin.

<*I had. I piggybacked on your records lookup. I wonder why they don't use it.*>

Nance pondered it as they took a lift up to the level where Jessica's stasis pod would be stored. <*Do you think that maybe they don't need to patrol the retro-zone much, so they don't fully staff stations here?*>

<*That would be a very, very interesting piece of intel,*> Erin replied with mental affirmation. <*I've wondered for some time how well Orion can maintain its fleets if they hold so much of their populace back at lower technology levels.*>

<*Me too,*> Nance replied. <*One thing's for certain, they sure breed a lot. From what Sera said about the Transcend,*

they have trouble growing their population. Only because no one dies does it stay stable.>

<Orion's people power vs the Transcend's technological might,> Erin observed. *<Somehow it's kept them in a three-thousand-year stalemate.>*

<Aided by distance. Hard to fight a war where the front is forty years across.>

Erin's avatar nodded in Nance's mind. *<Which is now moot with jump gates.>*

"Here we are," Colonel Ortaga said, disrupting Nance and Erin's conversation. "Secure Lockup C1."

They stood at a large door at the end of a short corridor. The door was set into a thick frame and didn't appear to have any visible hinges.

Ortaga stood still for a moment, passing his tokens, and then the security system reached out to Nance and Addie, requesting their tokens.

Finaeus and Iris had worked hard to extract the tokens from the captured Widows. It had taken some time, and he hadn't gained the assassin's more secure auths, but with luck the ones the team had would work for anything aboard Costa.

Nance held her breath as the room's security system ran her tokens. After a few seconds it came back with approval, and the door slowly slid sideways into the bulkhead.

"Very good," Nance said and walked into the room. A few cases rested against one wall, but otherwise the room was empty.

<I record receiving possession of the stasis pod containing Jessica Keller,> a voice—identified as belonging to an AI named Spheria—said over the Link.

"You are not taking possession," Nance said. "We are simply storing it here. A93 will remain with the pod and ensure it is safe."

Ortaga glanced back at Addie, who had not yet spoken once since they exited the *Sierra Echo*.

"Yes. I will remain with the pod," Addie said.

"Here. In the lockup?" Colonel Ortaga's voice was flat and disbelieving. "Won't you need to eat or anything?"

"No," Addie said.

Ortaga shrugged. "Suit yourself."

"I will accompany you to the command center," Nance said. "I have a message to send through the gate."

Ortaga looked between Nance and Addie, then down at the pod with Jessica within. "Very well. It's not far."

Nance nodded and followed the colonel back out of the secure lockup.

<The hackit is almost at the command center,> Erin reported to Nance as they walked out of the room and back to the lift. *<This AI they have here—>*

<Spheria?> Nance asked.

<Yeah, her. She's wily. I've caught her trying to probe us several times.>

<Does she suspect something?>

<I don't know,> Erin replied. *<She hasn't said anything, just keeps pushing at the edges, like she's trying to get something out of you.>*

Nance wondered if the Widows had some hidden trigger, or ident code they didn't know about. <*Is it safe to route a message to Iris? She may be able to tell.*>

<*I don't think so. If I route a message to the secure lockup, it has to go through Spheria. That defeats the purpose.*>

Nance examined the probes Spheria was making over the Link. It took a bit to understand what she was looking at, but it *was* a repeating pattern. A big one.

Nance ran it against the known Orion codes she'd gathered over the years, but didn't get any matches. Then she took the pattern from Spheria and ran it through a set of decryption algorithms, using the private keys they'd lifted from the Widows.

<*Why would she encrypt a message sent to you—well, A103?*> Erin wondered.

<*Beats me, I could barking up the wrong tree.*>

Nance spent another few seconds trying different algorithms, and then one clicked and the message from Spheria unfolded.

Are you in distress? Acknowledge.

<*Aw, crap! What do I do?*> Nance asked Erin.

<*Anything you send now will look suspect. You'd best ignore it. Maybe if she reaches—*>

Erin stopped as the lift stopped and the doors opened to reveal a squad of Orion Guard soldiers with weapons drawn.

<*Grab him!*> Erin shouted in Nance's mind, and she reacted instantly, grabbing Ortaga and pulling him into a back corner of the lift.

“Hold it! Let him go!” one of the soldiers shouted, but Nance was already in the lift controls, closing the doors and sending it up another level.

<*I knew it!*> Spheria cried out in Nance’s mind. <*You’re not A103, you’re an imposter.*>

<*Brilliant deduction,*> Nance replied sourly.

A second later the lift stopped, and then began to descend once more. At the same moment, Ortaga twisted and wrenched free of Nance’s grasp.

<*They’re onto us!*> Nance cried out to the team.

*****

Iris confirmed she had taken control of the secure lockup’s sensors and Jessica triggered the pod’s lid to open. She rose slowly, checking the room over. Addie stood next to the door, her helmeted head turned toward Jessica, watching implacably.

“Good work, Addie.”

“Impersonating these Widows is a simple task,” Addie replied. “Being you on the moons of Serenity was a much more challenging endeavor.”

Jessica wondered at Addie’s wording. An NSAI didn’t gain any joy from challenges, or lack thereof. They simply performed their assigned tasks.

She opened the compartment on the bottom of the pod and pulled out the weapons, and an Orion Guard uniform. She stepped into the pants and pulled the shirt over her head.

“It doesn’t fit right. I can tell you’re wearing your shipsuit underneath,” Addie observed.

"Yeah, well, this OG uniform has near-zero armor capability. My shipsuit stays. Not getting a hole burned in me today."

Addie cocked her head. "You expect conflict?"

"Yes."

Jessica pulled on the jacket that went along with her uniform and picked up the two rifles. She handed one to Addie, and then slung another over her back. She holstered a pistol, and then looked herself over.

"Your feet," Addie said, and Jessica laughed.

"Shit, must be nervous not to realize I'm barefoot," she muttered before fishing out the boots to go with her uniform.

<Really? Are you that nervous?> Iris asked.

<A bit, I guess,> Jessica said. *<This mission really has a do or die sort of feel to it.>*

<I get that,> Iris replied.

<Do you have an Ident for me?> Jessica asked.

<Yeah, I got into their personnel records on the way through the base—piggybacked off Addie to do it. You're now Lieutenant Mira. I've updated Addie with that information as well.>

<Good.> Jessica replied before speaking aloud. "Now to get out of here." She looked at the door and waved her arms. "Open Sesame!"

Nothing happened.

"I don't think that's the code," Addie said. "I also don't think it would be an audible command."

Jessica chuckled and gave Addie a curious look. "I thought you could parse humor, Addie."

"I wish you would stop making me break my persona," Addie replied. "I was in character."

Jessica's mouth formed an O as she gave a slow nod. "Hard to tell with the helmet."

Addy touched the sides of her collar and her helmet split open, revealing the face of a Widow. "I could take it off."

"Gah! No, only if you need to scare the piss out of some little Oggie."

"Understood," Addie rasped and closed her helmet back up.

<Ladies, we have a bit of a problem.> Iris said after a moment.

"That's the name of the game," Jessica replied. "What is it?"

<I can't get the door open.>

*****

<That's the third pair of guards to wander into the bay,> Cheeky said to Piya.

<And they're following a rather non-random pattern,> Piya replied. *<Each pair is moving closer to the ship, keeping in, or close to cover.>*

Cheeky nodded as she peered out the ship's front window to confirm what the external cameras showed.

<We need to get out of here. Should we risk a message to Nance and Jessica?>

<I don't think so,> Piya replied. *<They'll know we're suspicious if we do.>*

<Surely the Widows talk to one another,> Cheeky countered.

<Let's get out of the ship first. Then we won't be cornered if they know that we know what they're up to.>

Cheeky gave a soft laugh. *<You know that I know that you know that I think this is going to get messy.>*

<Har har. There was little chance that this mission was going to go off without a hitch,> Piya replied.

Cheeky nodded as she rose from her seat and looked out the window at another pair of soldiers strolling into the bay. "Mission, meet hitch."

The ship had a rear access port in the roof of its small engineering bay. Once Cheeky had grabbed a rifle and pistol from the armory, she clambered up the ladder and keyed in the code for the hatch.

The inner door slid open, and she quietly climbed the ladder into the small space between the two doors.

Here goes nuthin, Cheeky thought as she activated the Widow stealth systems. She looked down at her body and saw only a slight blur, like a dark patch in the air.

It was surprisingly difficult to key in the command for the external door without being able to see her hand, but then Piya activated an overlay mode on the helmet's HUD that showed the outline of her own body on her vision.

<Thanks.>

<Anytime, Cheeks.>

The hatch above sunk down a few centimeters, and then slid into the hull.

OK, now here ***really*** *goes nuthin',* Cheeky thought as she climbed up onto the roof of the ship. She stayed low, conscious of the turrets on the bay's ceiling, and somewhat surprised no one had seen her yet.

The hatch closed a moment later with a soft *ka-chunk* that sounded far too loud to Cheeky's ears and she moved away as quickly as she dared, toward the cooling vanes at the rear of the ship. They dipped low, only a few meters off the deck at the back, and a minute later, Cheeky was at the edge.

<*Coast looks as clear as it's going to get,*> Piya said and Cheeky jumped off the ship before she lost her nerve.

She landed lightly and rolled before coming back to her feet, looking around to see if anyone had noticed her.

So far, so good.

On the far side of the bay, she could make out more soldiers entering. At least sixteen were in the bay now.

<*I don't like these odds,*> Cheeky said to Piya.

<*So do what you did at Gisha Station,*> Piya replied.

It took Cheeky a moment to realize what Piya meant, and then she looked at the cradle. Sure enough, there was a ladder leading into the space below the deck. With any luck there'd be maintenance passages leading out of the bay.

<*Better than trying to sneak around half the Oggie space force,*> Cheeky said and crept to the ladder. She was half way down the ladder when a movement below caught her eye; four soldiers were threading their way through the cradle armature mounts below her.

She froze as one approached the ladder she was on and began to climb.

<*The side!*> Piya said. <*Hang off the side!*>

Cheeky swung over to the side of the ladder, planting her feet on the vertical riser and holding on for dear life.

The soldier was just below her now, and his hand barely missed her left foot. Given the distance he moved his hands each time, he was going to grab the riser right where her left hand held on.

She timed it carefully, and as he let go with his hand, she moved down, freeing up the space where her hand had been for his to grasp the ladder.

<*Shit, that was close!*> Cheeky exclaimed.

The soldier continued up the ladder and disappeared onto the deck. The other soldiers followed up other ladders, and Cheeky quickly scampered down to the lower service level.

<*At least we know there's a way out of here now,*> Piya offered.

<*So long as none of them are guarding it.*>

<*Jessica gave us nanocloud tech,*> Piya suggested as Cheeky crept through the cradle armatures.

<*Yeah, but do we want to tip our hand? They may not know who we are yet. Plus, I suck at controlling nanocloud. It always gets sucked into a vent or something.*>

Piya laughed and sent Cheeky a soothing feeling. <*I'll run them. You focus on stealth.*>

<*Easier said than done,*> Cheeky replied. <*My legs are too long and it's really messing me up. Who would have thought that three centimeters would change so much? The ground seems like it's too far away and I keep feeling like I'm going to fall forward.*>

<*I shouldn't do this, but its temporary,*> Piya said and suddenly everything felt properly aligned to Cheeky.

<Wow, that's way better. What'd you do?>

Piya grinned in Cheeky's mind. *<I altered the feeds in your ocular implants to lower your perceived eye level. Just be careful not to knock your head on things. It goes further up than it seems.>*

Cheeky reached up and had to keep going to find the top of her helmet. *<Gah, my head feels huge!>*

<You pick. Worry about falling, or feel like you have a big head.>

<Head it is,> Cheeky replied.

Cheeky caught sight of a passageway leading off the lower deck and a pair of soldiers standing guard.

<Shit!>

<Just walk right past them. It's dark down here, and I have the nanocloud hiding the slight shadow the Widow stealth has.>

Cheeky drew a slow breath, held it and walked toward the guards, careful to roll her feet and hold her arms still. The less air she moved around, the better the stealth would work.

The two guards never even twitched as she walked past, and a dozen meters into the passageway, Cheeky let out the breath. *<OK, the bay down, just a klick of station to go.>*

<I'm on the network,> Piya reported. *<There's a lockdown near the command center, and I can't reach Addie or Jess and Iris.>*

<Anything on the secure lockup?> Cheeky asked.

<Nothing on the general network, at least.>

Cheeky reviewed the best route to the lockup, and took off at a slow jog. She'd outpace the nanocloud, but she had a feeling speed trumped complete stealth at this point.

Ten minutes later, she eased into the short corridor that ended at the door to the secure lockup. The door was sealed shut, and Cheeky looked for some way to access its controls.

<*There's no panel or anything,*> she said to Piya.

<*I can see a scanning arch built into the wall. Step forward two paces and pass your tokens,*> Piya instructed.

Cheeky did as Piya directed and then a voice came into her mind.

<*Got you!*>

<*Shit, that's the station AI, Spheria,*> Piya said. <*She's serious business from what I sensed. Not like most of the AI we've met up with out here.*>

Cheeky didn't respond to the AI, but knew she should expect soldiers to show up at any moment.

Then the secure lockup's door opened, and Addie stepped out with an Orion soldier at her side. A very curvaceous Orion soldier.

"Jessica?" Cheeky asked the dark-haired woman.

"Yeah, I can't just run around all purple on base—wait, A45? What are you doing here?"

<*The game's up,*> Piya said. <*Station AI is on to us. I can't reach Nance, though the hackit did make it to the command center—but now it's out of touch.*>

<*Oh, this Spheria is a nasty bit of work,*> Iris broke into the conversation. <*Going to enjoy putting her in her place.*>

"OK, Cheeky, you and Addie get to their central command. See what's up with the hackit and get it

Linked into the gate control. I'm going to go hunt down Nance."

Cheeky felt herself pale…not that anyone could see it behind the helmet. "Really? You sure we should split up?"

Jessica stepped forward and put a hand on Cheeky's shoulder. "We're already split up. Don't doubt yourself because of one little abduction. It happens to the best of us. It's just two levels up. You can do this."

<*Just don't take the lifts,*> Iris advised.

"Oh," Jessica pulled the pack off her back. "Take the explosives as well. Once you get the gate lined up, you know what to do."

Cheeky nodded. "OK, Addie, let's go."

BAD TO WORSE

STELLAR DATE: 03.22.8948 (Adjusted Years)
LOCATION: Costa Station, Quera System
REGION: Midway Cluster, Orion Freedom Alliance Space

<What do you have, Iris?> Jessica asked as she watched Cheeky's and Addie's shadows disappear down the corridor.

She was half-tempted to take off the Oggie uniform. Since stealth was no longer the name of the game, shock and awe may work better.

Then again, a moment's pause from any Oggies she saw could be the difference between life and death.

<I've taken control of the subnet on this level and have blinded Spheria down here. She's a really testy thing, but everything she's throwing at me is stuff that Angela dealt with back in Sol and gave me counters for.>

<Strange how they use so much old tech,> Jessica said as she made her way to the lift.

<They don't call our time the golden age for nothing. Hey, I thought we were avoiding the lifts.>

Jessica prised the lift doors open and looked into the shaft. *<We're not taking the lift, per se, just the shaft. Which way did Nance go? Up or down?>*

Iris didn't respond for a second, then laughed. *<She's down. Looks like Spheria got wise to her, set an ambush, and Nance dropped the lift down to the maintenance levels. From the reports on their network, she has Colonel Ortaga hostage.>*

<Can you reach her?>

<No, Spheria has the network between here and there, but I think Nance and Erin are fighting her too. She seems…distracted.>

Jessica looked for a ladder in the lift shaft, but there was none, just a rail that maintenance bots traversed.

"Looks like I'm going for a slide," she said softly, glad for the gloves that were a part of the standard Oggie uniform.

She slid for fifteen levels before the gloves began to heat up and tear, and then went hand over hand for the last twenty down to the maintenance levels where Iris believed Nance to be.

<Next one, level 17,> Nance informed Jessica as she descended.

<Thank stars, this is exhausting.>

At the specified level, Jessica swung out and pulled the doors open, peering down the—thankfully—empty corridor.

<Got them!> Iris called out. *<Hi Erin.>*

<Stars! Glad to see you got out! Where's Cheeky?> Nance asked.

<Hopefully at the command center by now. We need to get back up too.>

The sounds of weapons fire echoed down the corridor before Nance replied.

<Love to, but there's a whole fucking 'toon of Oggies down here. Good thing I have Ortaga as a human shield. They must like him or something.>

<On my way,> Jessica replied as Iris pinpointed Nance's location on the level.

She sprinted down the passageway and passed into a large room. The overhead lay ten meters above, and tanks filled the area. The sounds of pumps, liquid sloshing, and a dozen other noises she couldn't readily identify assaulted her.

Great, ambush central.

Jessica flushed out a passel of nano as she skirted around the edge of the room, rifle stock tight against her shoulder as she worked her way past the rows of tanks and pipes.

Movement behind a tank caught Jessica's attention, and she quickly backtracked to take cover behind a cluster of pipes rising up out of the deck.

She flipped her rifle from pulse shots to its fifteen millimeter explosive tip rounds and took aim at a pipe feeding into one of the tanks.

A long exhale, a trigger squeeze, and the pipe exploded, spraying human waste into the space below. There was a cry of dismay, and Jessica rushed around the clean side of the tank to see two soldiers backing away from the filth.

Two shots later and they were down.

Jessica circled around the tanks and took a new route down the center of the room. She caught sight of two guards a moment before they saw her, and they joined their comrades in the afterlife.

<I have the room covered with nano, now. There are six other Oggies here, but they're working around the far side. They think you're still along the bulkheads.>

<Good,> Jessica replied as she reached the exit on the far side. *<Seal them in.>*

Iris closed off the exit behind Jessica and she continued along her route to Nance.

<Backed into a corner here, Jess. Could really use an assist soon,> Nance called in.

<Almost there, I'll be on their asses in thirty seconds.>

Jessica rounded a corner and spotted a squad of Oggies crouched along the edges of the corridor. She pulled her pistol free and opened fire with both weapons, tearing into the enemy's backs and mowing down four before they'd even turned.

There were still ten of the enemy in the passageway, and half of them turned and fired on Jessica, who ducked back behind the corner.

She lobbed a grenade around the corner at the same time that shots joined in from the far end of the passageway.

There was a thundering explosion, and then silence reigned.

Jessica eased around the corner and sighed as Nance emerged from the smoke.

Nance threaded her way through the bodies of the enemy, and one groaned as Nance walked past. The ship's engineer casually shot the soldier in the head.

The action surprised Jessica. Not that *she* wouldn't have done it—they couldn't afford to leave enemies behind them—but she'd never seen Nance do anything like that.

"Where's the colonel?" Jessica asked as Nance reached her.

"He didn't make it," Nance replied in her unnerving Widow's voice. "Turns out his people didn't like him as much as I'd thought."

Jessica couldn't tell if it was the ethereal sound of Nance's words, or something else, but she wasn't entirely certain if Nance had told her the truth.

She quashed her worry for the time being. "Less to worry about then. We have to get up to the CC."

<*I've reconnected with the network on the upper levels,*> Iris said. <*Cheeky and Addie made it in, but they're trapped now.*>

"What about the jump gate?" Nance asked.

<*I don't know, I don't have external sensor access—yet.*>

* * * * *

<Sabrina, *come in* Sabrina!>

Cargo almost leapt out of his seat with joy when Cheeky's voice came in over the comm system.

<*Cheeky! The station is throwing up alerts like mad, have you been made?*>

<*Oh, hell yeah. Made with a side of holy shit. Jessica is trying to rescue Nance, but Addie and I are in the command center. The hackit got here and it's interfaced with the gate control. Thing is, the gate control system is…I don't know, it's whack. The hackit can't feed in the coordinates. Piya and I can't make heads or tails of it either.*>

Cargo glanced at Finaeus who rose from his seat, staring at Costa station on the forward display. <*OK, Cheeky, let me piggyback through. I'll see what I can do.*>

<*You got it,*> Cheeky replied.

<You two safe in there?> Cargo asked.

<Relative term,> Cheeky replied after a brief pause. *<Addie went all extreme prejudice on the crew working in here—orders from Jessica I guess—but the Oggies chasing us got a detpack on the doors, so they're half blown open right now.>*

<What about the station's external fire control?> Cargo asked.

<Offline. Hackit had no problem with that.>

<OK. I'm sending Trevor over now,> Cargo said. *<Once Finaeus gets the gate programmed, you hold out 'til Trevor shows.>*

<With bated breath!>

Cargo sent the signal to Trevor. A moment later, the pinnace separated from *Sabrina* and boosted toward the station.

<OK, I've got the gate realigning,> Finaeus said a moment later.

<Good. Let's—> He stopped as the Orion Guard destroyer pulled away from Costa's docking ring. *<Trevor, you're about to get some company.>*

<I see it, I'll loop around Costa. Can you take it?>

<Can I take it?> Sabrina muttered. *<Really, Trevor? Haven't you seen my teeth?>*

Trevor laughed over the Link. *<Just goosing you up, Sabs. Kick some ass.>*

A holo appeared in the pilot's seat. It was the female figure Sabrina often used as her Avatar over the Link. She turned and winked at Cargo.

"I figured that would be more comfortable for you. Plus, I want to see if it helps me fly with my gut."

Cargo shook his head as he sat back down in the command chair. "Let's give that destroyer hell."

* * * * *

Cheeky ducked down behind a console as weapons fire poured into the command center. "Shit, these assholes just won't give up!"

"Yes, I don't think they have any intention of giving up," Addie said as she moved to a new position and fired through the CC's half-ruined doors.

Cheeky sighed and glanced back at the holodisplay that showed space around Costa and the jump gate. *Sabrina* was visible on it, now, leading the destroyer away from the station while the SS *Sexy* made its approach to the airlock near the command center.

"Time to blow some shit up," she muttered and opened up the satchel with the detpacks.

<Put one on either side of the room. Over by those support columns,> Piya said. *<That should blow the command center clear off the station.>*

Cheeky chuckled. "Gonna be real hard to re-align the gate with the CC gone."

<So long as Iris and Erin can shut down that Spheria. She's a real bitch.>

<There's only one comm array that can talk to the gate, and it's directly attached to the CC here,> Piya replied. *<Once we blow this joint, the gate is locked down. Spheria or no Spheria.>*

"Good," Cheeky said as she moved from cover to cover. Addie kept up the pressure and Cheeky reached the left side of the room without incident, planting the detpack against the support column.

She looked across the command center, gauging the best route to the other support column when an explosion shook the deck and Cheeky spun to see more of the door rent wide. Smoke filled the entrance, and the enemy fire slackened for a moment.

"Shit!" she swore.

<*Go now!*> Piya shouted and Cheeky dashed across the command center, keeping low while Addie sprayed covering fire through doorway.

Cheeky was a meter from her destination when a spray of kinetic slugs tore through the air. She dove low, sliding across the floor and scampering behind the column.

<*Cheeky!*> Piya shouted, and at the same time she saw the red streak Cheeky had left on the floor.

"Can't look yet," Cheeky muttered as she set the detpack at the base of the column and armed it.

<*Cheeky, the armor, it can't…*> Piya exclaimed in dismay.

Cheeky finally looked down at her body a gave a soft shuddering gasp. The left side of her abdomen was a bloody ruin.

"Holy shit!" she screamed as pain slammed into her, followed by a sudden wave of dizziness.

<*Your neck, you got hit in the neck too!*>

Cheeky put a hand to her neck and pulled it back looking at the blood flowing down her arm. "Whoa…that's a lot…"

Addie was beside her a second later, firing her rifle at the door, explosive tipped rounds shredding anything in their path as she applied biofoam to Cheeky's neck.

"There's too many out there," Addie said and Cheeky was certain she heard worry in the AHAP's voice. "I only have one mag after this."

<Cheeky. Your batts got hit, we're on reserves.>

<I guess this is how we go, Piya. At least we got the gate lined up. Sabs and everyone will get to go home.>

<No!> Piya shouted in Cheeky's mind. *<Not again, not like this! We survived the black holes at Grey Wolf, we can survive this.>*

Cheeky tried to lift her rifle to fire toward the door, but it was just too heavy. Shots tore through a nearby console, and she barely had the strength to flinch.

Addie dropped her rifle and grabbed Cheeky's, opening fire once more.

<Stay conscious, just a little longer,> Piya said in a strange tone—almost pleading—but her voice sounded tinged with hope.

Something felt strange, memories of her life kept flashing through Cheeky's mind. Most seemed to be from the past eighteen years, and emotions assaulted Cheeky as she relived what felt like half her life in under a minute.

<Am I dying? Is my life flashing before my eyes?>

<No, I'm saving you—saving us.>

A moment later a burst of energy came over her, as though something that had been sapping her energy was gone.

<Piya?> Cheeky cried out, but there was no response. *<Piya! Where are you?>*

Addie was looking at Cheeky with her black-helmeted head tilted to the side. "Hold on just a bit longer. Don't let them disarm the detpacks."

Addie passed her pistol to Cheeky and then drew Cheeky's own and placed it in her other hand.

"Don't let them through," Addie said in the breathy rasp of a Widow. "Cover me."

Cheeky didn't understand what the AHAP was saying. "What? You're supposed to cover me!"

An explosion flared beyond the doors and Addie rose up, rushing toward the exit, rifle tucked against her shoulder, firing controlled bursts.

Then Addie was gone, lost in the smoke from the explosion.

* * * * *

Jessica skidded to a halt as the entrance to the command center came into view. At least two-dozen Oggie soldiers were clustered around the half-ruined doors, shooting into the command center while a smattering of return fire came out.

<Crap!> Nance exclaimed and ducked behind the corner while Jessica crossed the corridor.

<Ready? On three…two…one!>

Easing out from cover, the two women opened fire on the soldiers, tearing into their ranks. The Oggies up here were wearing better armor than those below, and only three dropped before half the enemy spun and returned fire.

<*There's too many!*> Nance exclaimed.

"Need an assist?" a voice said from behind Jessica and she spun to see a hulking figure in heavy-powered armor lumber into view.

"Trevor!" Jessica exclaimed. "Yes, quick! Cheeky and Addie are trapped down there. I can't seem to reach either of them on the Link, but there's shots coming out."

Trevor was already moving as Jessica spoke, swinging a kinetic chain gun out into the corridor and opening fire on the Oggie soldiers. Five went down in the opening salvo, and then something exploded in the corridor and the space was filled with smoke.

<*Hold fire!*> Jessica shouted as a black figure sprinted out of the command center, past the stunned Oggie soldiers.

It was a Widow, but Jessica couldn't tell if it was Cheeky or Addie.

"We gotta go!" the figure called out, and Jessica's HUD registered the figure as Addie.

The AHAP ducked around the corner and Jessica grabbed her arm. "You left her!" Jessica screamed. "What did you do, Addie?"

"She ordered me to go," Addie said. "I had to save her!"

"No!" Nance screamed, racing down the corridor, firing wildly at the Oggie soldiers while Trevor covered her with his chaingun.

"Fuck!" Jessica swore and took off after Nance.

Several Oggie soldiers turned to open fire on her, but Jessica unleashed blasts of energy from her hands at each, taking out one after another until her Retyna gauge hit zero.

A shot from Trevor took out the last of the enemy soldiers and Jessica sprinted on. Her longer legs gave her enough speed to catch up to Nance at the entrance to the command center. She scanned the area, looking for Cheeky. Jessica's heart leapt into her throat when she caught sight of Cheeky slumped against a column on the right side of the room. Her helmet was off and a pair of dead Oggie soldiers lay at her feet.

"Cheeky!" Jessica cried out and swung a leg over the ruin of the door.

"No! Jessica! *Go!*" Cheeky screamed, blood spraying out of her mouth.

Nance was right beside Jessica, half straddling the ruined door. "Cheeky! We're coming for you!"

"*Go!* It's gonna blow!" Cheeky shrieked and waved her arms frantically.

Jessica took an involuntary step forward—she couldn't abandon her friend. Not here, not after they'd been through so much.

Then fire consumed the command center.

The force of the explosion picked Jessica up and threw her back into the corridor where she slammed into a bulkhead, cracking the back of her head against a beam.

Her vision swam as a secondary *SHOOM* thundered through the corridor and her ears popped. She struggled to her feet while everything around her sounded like it was underwater—or she was underwater.

A wind pulled at her, dragging her to the end of the corridor and Jessica knew that was bad—but that's where Cheeky was. She had to save Cheeky.

<Jessica! No!> Iris screamed in her mind, and she wondered why the AI didn't want to save Cheeky. Wasn't Iris in love with Piya?

Then a strong hand clamped around her arm and another wrapped around her torso. She was pressed up against something black. Was it Cheeky? No, Cheeky's helmet had been off, she distinctly remembered that.

<She's gone, Jessica! She's gone! Stop fighting,> Trevor yelled in her mind and Jessica became aware she'd been flailing her limbs.

She's gone…Cheeky's gone….

She went limp, all her energy gone as Trevor carried her and Nance down a corridor and through an airlock.

With a start, Jessica realized they were in the *Sexy* and tried to pull free from Trevor. "Trevor!" she said, her voice sounding strange.

<Your eardrums popped,> Iris said. *<From the depressurization. But Cheeky made sure the command center blew. The gate's aligned, they can't stop us now.>*

Hot tears spilled down Jessica's face as she screamed something even she didn't understand while beating her fist against the bulkhead.

She heard cursing next to her, saw that Nance was trying to get her helmet off. Jessica reached out and helped her, the helmet split apart a moment later and Nance's tear-streaked face came into view.

Jessica didn't know what to say, and gathered Nance into her arms as a loud clang heralded the *Sexy*'s departure from Costa station.

<I'm so sorry,> Jessica whispered into Nance's mind. *<I—>*

<Jessica,> Iris whispered. *<Trevor needs your help, he can't do this piloting on his own. It's a mess out here.>*

Jessica nodded. She had a duty to perform. She knew how to do that. As she rose, her gaze fell on Addie's motionless form next to Nance. A hole had been blown clear through the AHAP's torso, and her left leg was missing.

"Fucking machine! Why'd you leave her?" Jessica swore and kicked Addie. She didn't move, and Jessica wiped the tears from her face before turning toward the cockpit.

She slid into a seat beside Trevor, trying to control her breathing as she took stock of the situation. The holodisplay showed Costa behind them and the jump gate ahead. *Sabrina* was to their starboard, firing its beams at the OG destroyer, while Trevor jinked the *Sexy*, avoiding beamfire from the two patrol craft near the gate.

"You got it?" Trevor asked. "I'll take the beams."

Jessica glanced at Trevor, noting the concern in his eyes.

"Yeah, I got it,"

She took control of the ship, dumping it into a corkscrew spin before veering off, cutting across the bows of the two patrol craft, giving Trevor clear shots, which he took, blowing one of the enemy ships out of the black.

<Nice shooting,> Iris said. *<But we gotta get linked up with* Sabrina. *The OG fleet is back and they're closing in fast.>*

Jessica looked at the long-range scan which displayed over a hundred cruisers and destroyers bearing down on Costa station. They were still out of effective beam range, but wouldn't be in just a few minutes.

"Why can't we get a fucking break?" Jessica swore and punched a console.

"Stay on target," Trevor said. "Link us up and we jump out."

Jessica looked at the gate. It was active, ready for *Sabrina*'s bow-mirror to touch the roiling not-space at the center of the ring and send them home.

Home…. Jessica could find no meaning in the word as she spun the *Sexy* and boosted back toward *Sabrina*. Beyond the starfreighter, the enemy destroyer began to split and then cracked in half, gouts of fire bursting into space as the Oggie ship burned to death.

"Die, motherfuckers," Jessica whispered as she lined the *Sexy* up with *Sabrina. <Sabs, hold vector for twenty more seconds. Then we'll be locked on.>*

<I found my gut!> Sabrina called back. *<I'm flying with my gut!>*

Jessica wanted to congratulate Sabrina, but the words wouldn't come.

<Good,> Trevor replied on her behalf. *<We'll be there in a moment.>*

Jessica put all her focus into bringing the *Sexy* down onto *Sabrina*'s back where the small cradle and ship-to-ship airlock waited.

She hit the armatures hard, and nearly bounced off, but then *Sabrina* pulled them into place with a grav field and the armatures made grapple.

<Locked and loaded,> Trevor called out. *<Take us through, Sabs.>*

<You got it,> Sabrina crowed, her voice gleeful as the ship turned, arcing through space to the jump gate.

Jessica heard a sound from behind her and turned to see Nance standing beside her seat. She reached out a hand and Nance clasped it while Trevor reached over and placed a hand on Jessica's thigh.

None of them moved or spoke as the jump gate grew larger and larger. They saw *Sabrina's* mirror flow out from the bow of the ship and then time seemed to slow as it met the energy on the gate's focal line.

Then everything disappeared.

3KPC

STELLAR DATE: 03.22.8948 (Adjusted Years)
LOCATION: *Sabrina*
REGION: Unknown Location, Milky Way Galaxy

"Were the missiles on target?" Cargo asked, the moment space disappeared around them.

"They were lined up," Finaeus replied. "Those asshats won't even see them until the last second. Then their gate goes poof."

Finaeus splayed his fingers and spread his hands through the air to emphasize his point.

"You sure the relativistic missiles can take out the gate?" Misha asked.

Finaeus snorted. "Misha, my boy. That's the thing about jump gates. They're fragile. Especially while they're on. Even if one of those RMs detonates within a thousand klicks, that gate's done. Probably take out half of Costa when it goes, too."

<You secure?> Cargo called up to the *Sexy*.

<Yeah, we're locked on. Coming down now,> Trevor replied. There was something in his voice Cargo didn't like. A sinking feeling settled into the pit of his stomach.

He wanted to ask who or what, but didn't want to know at the same time.

<Noooooo…> Sabrina wailed suddenly, broadcasting her distress to everyone aboard. *<Why aren't Cheeky and Piya responding? Are they hurt?>*

Cargo caught Finaeus's eye and they shared a look of fear before Jessica responded.

<Cheeky and Piya…> Jessica's voice came a moment later. *<They held on 'til the end. Made sure the bastards couldn't realign the gate.>*

Cargo felt a lump form in his throat as Sabrina wailed audibly and Finaeus collapsed into a chair. Misha rose, tears streaming down his face, and took a few halting steps to Finaeus and knelt beside the ancient man before wrapping his arms around him.

Cargo lost track of time as they waited for the rest of the team to arrive. It felt like forever, but it was still too soon when Jessica, Trevor, and Nance shuffled onto the bridge.

Nance rushed to Cargo and wrapped her arms around him, and the pair held one another for several minutes. He was dimly aware of soft murmurs as the other members of the crew spoke, and the AIs lamented.

Then something occurred to Cargo and his head snapped up from Nance's shoulder.

"Finaeus, it's been ten minutes…it didn't take this long to get to Perseus. Have we overshot New Canaan?"

Finaeus rose from his seat and walked to the front of the bridge, wiping his cheeks with the back of his hands as he went. "I realized that we couldn't jump right to New Canaan. It was too risky. Orion may have worked out the system's coordinates. We're going somewhere else first."

"Where?" Cargo growled. "Where have you taken us?"

"You'll seeee…now." Finaeus said wearily as normal space snapped into place around them once more.

Except it wasn't normal.

Brilliant starlight lit up the display at the front of the bridge—a sight like nothing Cargo had ever seen before. Not even the largest star clusters were this bright.

"Where are we?" Jessica asked softly.

"Jelina Arm…at least that's what I call it," Finaeus replied tonelessly. "The common name is still the 3KPC Arm—which is stupid."

"What?" Cargo shouted as he stepped away from Nance, looming over Finaeus. "That's almost at the galactic core! What have you done, you old fool? I—"

<*Wait, Cargo,*> Sabrina interrupted. <*There's something here, a structure…*>

"I had been building this place in secret," Finaeus said as he brought up the object on the holo. "Using machines, not people. No AI either. It looks like they finished, which is good for us."

"You have an outpost fifteen thousand light years beyond New Canaan?" Jessica asked, her voice filled with wonder. "Why?"

"Well, we're only about fourteen thousand light years from New Canaan. Just on the edge of the Galactic Bar. Sagittarius A* is only about five thousand light years from here."

"So it's a science outpost?" Nance asked. "You were going to study the galactic core?"

Finaeus snorted. "Yeah, sorta. I was going to send an expedition in. This was to be my staging ground."

He waved a hand at the holo, and the structure Sabrina had spotted—which was in orbit of a terrestrial planet with a dim red star beyond—came into sharper view.

Cargo drew in a long breath. “It has a gate.”

“Yes,” Finaeus nodded. “It has a gate.”

“Let’s…” Jessica started to say, then her voice failed her for a moment. She swallowed, and then continued. “Let’s not go to New Canaan just yet.”

“It’ll take a day to get down there anyway,” Cargo said.

“And I need to get put back the way I was,” Nance added quietly. “I don’t want to look like this for another second.”

Finaeus let out a long breath, then asked the question that was on Cargo’s mind as well. “Did you bring them…the body…back?”

Jessica bit her lip and shook her head before whispering, “No.”

“Is there any chance?” Finaeus asked.

“No,” Jessica repeated. “They’re gone.”

“But how…?” Cargo asked.

“It was that core-damned machine, the AHAP,” Nance said, vitriol spilling from her lips. “She just *left* Cheeky!”

“Did she say—” Finaeus began, but Jessica shook her head again.

“Just said that ‘she’ told her to go as she ran past me. Then the stupid AHAP got shot to shit too.”

Misha walked onto the bridge with a bottle of vodka and a stack of glasses. “A drink,” he said. “Where I come from, it’s our tradition to toast someone who’s passed as soon as the news is received.”

The crewmembers all nodded silently, and the AIs appeared as holoprojections in their midst. Hank, Iris,

Erin, and Sabrina. All looking as sorrowful and morose as the humans they stood amongst.

Misha passed the glasses out and poured a drink for each, while already filled cups appeared in the hands of the AIs.

Cargo knew it fell to him to say the words. He just didn't know what they should be. The lump in his throat had returned as he realized Cheeky—that smiling, happy woman—would never be in the pilot's seat again.

It would never be the same.

"I—" he began and then his voice failed him. The hand holding the glass shook for a moment and he feared the drink would spill before the toast.

Cargo took a deep breath and managed to find his voice. "I still remember the first day I met her. Sera had just hired me on as the first mate. When I stepped onto the bridge, Cheeky was standing there wearing her "Got Milk" shirt…and what I first thought was her underwear—"

Cargo laughed and several of the crew joined in.

He drew another breath and swallowed the lump back down once more. "Sera introduced her as the heart of the ship, and it didn't take me long to realize what she meant. Cheeky was the heart of all of us. She and Piya were kindred spirits that made everyone around them feel better about themselves and life…I'm going to miss them both more than I can say."

Following his words, everyone was silent, then Nance said her piece, followed by Trevor. One-by-one everyone on the crew spoke a few words. Everyone except for Sabrina.

The ship's AI stood next to Cargo, staring down at the holographic glass she held for over a minute before she looked up at the rest of the crew.

"She was my soulmate," the AI whispered. "I'll miss her forever."

HERE TO THERE

STELLAR DATE: 03.27.8948 (Adjusted Years)
LOCATION: *Sabrina*
REGION: Jelina System, 3KPC Arm, Milky Way Galaxy

Five days later…

Jessica sat in the pilot's seat, staring at the jump gate as it grew larger in the forward view, the roiling ball of twisted space—or whatever it really was—in its center.

She shifted uncomfortably. It didn't feel right. She'd sat in this seat a thousand times before, but it just didn't feel right.

Her gaze fell to her hands; boring, a matte lavender color, no glow to be seen.

<Finaeus thinks he might be able to fix you, you know,> Iris said in a soft tone. *<We still have that tank of Retyna product from back at Hermes Station.>*

<That's not the same product, though,> Jessica replied. *<Not like what they'd put in my skin.>*

Her overuse of the microbe's charge in that final push to reach Cheeky had killed off the colonies of alien bacteria living in Jessica's artificial skin. She didn't glow anymore, and her skin felt numb, with barely any tactile sensation.

Insult to injury.

<We'll be at New Canaan soon,> Iris said, trying to be comforting. *<Then we'll be back on the* Intrepid*…or wherever.>*

<Will leaving this ship make anything better? I'll just feel like I'm abandoning Sabrina.>

Iris was silent for a minute, then she said, *<I know…I have no idea what is the right thing.>*

The display before Jessica lit up, showing a lock on the jump gate.

"We're lined up. Taking us in," she announced quietly.

"New Canaan this time, right, Finaeus?" Cargo asked and Jessica gave a soft laugh.

"Yeah, New Canaan. No shenanigans, I promise."

"About time," Jessica said as she increased thrust, pushing the ship forward.

"Deploying the mirror," Finaeus announced.

Jessica held her breath as the shimmering silver mirror appeared before the ship, supported before them by a stasis bubble. A moment later it touched the gate's ball of energy, and they jumped.

No one spoke for the duration. Nearly seven minutes of silence stretched out as their tiny bit of normal matter skipped across the underlying fabric of the universe—or wherever they really were.

"Annnd, mark," Finaeus said as the stars snapped into view around them once more—one quite a bit brighter than the rest.

They were in a star system at least, hopefully it was actually New Canaan this time.

Jessica brought up scan and surveyed the system they were in, looking for a sign that they had come to the right place.

"Well?" Cargo asked. "Are we there?"

"What the…?!" Jessica exclaimed as she spotted two massive fleets in a stand-off near one of the system's gas giants. "Is there some sort of party going on here that we didn't know about?"

*****

On deck of the *Sexy*, still laying where Trevor had dumped her, Addie felt the small shift of a grav-dampened acceleration. It was a hard burn and she wondered what was going on.

She also wondered why no one had come for her after they made it back to *Sabrina.* It had been days.

And she carried something very important….

THE END

*****

Thus ends *Sabrina*'s journey through Orion Space.

These six books of Perseus Gate Season 1: Orion Space take place during the latter half of the book, *New Canaan*. And while it may feel like an ending, it is really a beginning.

If you have held off, now is the time to read *Orion Rising*, and if you have already read Orion Rising, then you can begin Book 1 of Perseus Gate Season 2: Inner Stars.

That story starts just one day after *Sabrina* arrives in New Canaan and will see the crew off on a new adventure, where they must stop the AI uprising they inadvertently started eighteen years prior in Virginis.

Thank you for taking this journey with me through the Perseus Gate. You've all made it tremendously successful—more than I'd ever dreamed—and have ensured that tales of Jessica, Sabrina, and the rest of the crew will continue for some time.

Continue the story in *Orion Rising*
Jump to Season 2 in *A Meeting of Minds and Bodies*

THE BOOKS OF AEON 14

Keep up to date with what is releasing in Aeon 14 with the free Aeon 14 Reading Guide.

The Intrepid Saga
- Book 1: Outsystem
- Book 2: A Path in the Darkness
- Book 3: Building Victoria

- The Intrepid Saga Omnibus – *Also contains Destiny Lost, book 1 of the Orion War series*

- Destiny Rising – *Special Author's Extended Edition comprised of both Outsystem and A Path in the Darkness with over 100 pages of new content.*

The Orion War
- Book 1: Destiny Lost
- Book 2: New Canaan
- Book 3: Orion Rising
- Book 4: The Scipio Alliance
- Book 5: Attack on Thebes (Feb 2018)
- Book 6: The Thousand Front War (2018)
- Book 7: Fallen Empire
- Many more following

Tales of the Orion War
- Book 1: Set the Galaxy on Fire
- Book 2: Ignite the Stars (Feb 2018)
- Book 3: Burn the Galaxy to Ash (2018)

Perilous Alliance (Age of the Orion War - with Chris J. Pike)
- Book 1: Close Proximity
- Book 2: Strike Vector
- Book 3: Collision Course

- Impact Immanent (2018)

Rika's Marauders (Age of the Orion War)
- Prequel: Rika Mechanized
- Book 1: Rika Outcast
- Book 2: Rika Redeemed
- Book 3: Rika Triumphant (2018)
- Book 4: Rika Commander (2018)
- Book 5: Rika Unleashed (2018)

Perseus Gate (Age of the Orion War)
Season 1: Orion Space
- Episode 1: The Gate at the Grey Wolf Star
- Episode 2: The World at the Edge of Space
- Episode 3: The Dance on the Moons of Serenity
- Episode 4: The Last Bastion of Star City
- Episode 5: The Toll Road Between the Stars
- Episode 6: The Final Stroll on Perseus's Arm
- Eps 1-3 Omnibus: The Trail Through the Stars
- Eps 4-6 Omnibus: The Path Amongst the Clouds

Season 2: The Inner Stars
- Episode 1: A Meeting of Bodies and Minds (Feb 2018)
- More coming in 2018

The Warlord (Before the Age of the Orion War)
- Book 1: The Woman Without a World
- Book 2: The Woman Who Seized an Empire
- Book 3: The Woman Who Lost Everything (March 2018)

The Sentience Wars: Origins (With James S. Aaron)
- Book 1: Lyssa's Dream
- Book 2: Lyssa's Run
- Book 3: Lyssa's Flight (Jan 2018)
- Book 4: Lyssa's Call (2018)
- Book 5: Lyssa's Flame (2018)

Machete System Bounty Hunter (Age of the Orion War - with Zen DiPietro)
- Book 1: Hired Gun (Feb 2018)
- More coming in 2018

The Empire (Age of the Orion War)
- The Empress and the Ambassador (2018)
- Consort of the Scorpion Empress (2018)
- By the Empress's Command (2018)

Tanis Richards: Origins
- Prequel: Storming the Norse Wind (At the Helm Volume 3)
- Book 1: Shore Leave (June 2018)
- Book 2: The Command (June 2018)
- Book 3: Infiltrator (July 2018)

The Sol Dissolution
- The 242 - Venusian Uprising (The Expanding Universe 2 anthology)
- The 242 - Assault on Tarja (The Expanding Universe 3 anthology)

The Delta Team Chronicles (Expanded Orion War)
- A "Simple" Kidnapping (Pew! Pew! Volume 1)
- The Disknee World (Pew! Pew! Volume 2)
- It's Hard Being a Girl (Pew! Pew! Volume 4)
- A Fool's Gotta Feed (Pew! Pew! Volume 4)

ABOUT THE AUTHOR

Michael Cooper likes to think of himself as a jack-of-all-trades (and hopes to become master of a few). When not writing, he can be found writing software, working in his shop at his latest carpentry project, or likely reading a book.

He shares his home with a precocious young girl, his wonderful wife (who also writes), two cats, a never-ending list of things he would like to build, and ideas...

Find out what's coming next at http://www.aeon14.com

Made in the USA
Middletown, DE
06 January 2018